ALBATROSS

Clash of the Most Notorious
Killer and Golfer of Their Time

ALBATROSS

SCOTT N. GARDNER

PALMETTO
PUBLISHING
Charleston, SC
www.PalmettoPublishing.com

Paperback ISBN: 979-8-8229-4358-2
eBook ISBN: 979-8-8229-4359-9

This is a work of historical fiction, and although many of the locations, events, and people are real, including the Overland Country Club, the Ten Bells Pub, the Estes Park Hotel, the Queen Mary, the Canonical Five murders, the Golf Exhibition, Harry Vardon's funeral, Jack the Ripper, Harry Vardon, Henry Wolcott, Walter Fairbanks, and Walter Hagen. However, Charlie Swafford, Camille Hawthbaren, the Cuddlings, and Catherine George are fictional. The plot is the imagination of the author, and the author makes no claim as to historic fact.

My knife's so nice and sharp. I want to get to work right away!
—Jack the Ripper

I'm the best, and I'll thank you for remembering that!
—Harry Vardon

CONTENTS

CONTENTS CONTINUED

PROLOGUE

It was the stroke of midnight on January 1, 1888. Two witches, one good and one evil, sat around a cauldron of herbs, roots, and horse hoofs and selected magical mushrooms.

"Your turn to stir," the Good Witch said to the evil one, passing over the long wooden ladle.

"What is your handicap these nights?" the Evil Witch asked the good one.

"I am down to ten; took a lesson from Old Tom Morris last week. How about you?" the Good Witch asked the evil one.

"I am a six, but as you know, I cheat a lot."

The Good Witch agreed with that statement with a nod of the head.

"Look, things are coming into focus," said the Bad Witch, pulling the ladle from the clearing concoction.

There, rising to the top, was the figure of a man walking down a cobblestone street in the Whitechapel district of London.

"What kind of evil scheming are you up to?" the Good Witch asked.

"I was just thinking the other night when I was out walking my black cats that I have not done anything really evil as of late. As you know I have a reputation to uphold," said the Bad Witch.

The Good Witch countered by asking, "Is there not enough calamity in the world already?"

The Bad Witch continued, "I am only asking for five murders—well, actually six. I lose count sometimes.

"You really need a vacation, you know that?" the Good Witch said, then continued on, "As usual, all I can do to counter your wickedness is add a silver lining where I can. Now can we eat? I am starving," said the Good Witch.

CHAPTER ONE
VARDON'S COMING

Denver, Colorado, October 6, 1900

Reginald Hawthbaren, President of the Denver Tramway Company, eased himself down onto a plush leather chair situated in the Trophy Room of the Denver Club. Established in 1880 and located at Seventeenth Street and Glenarm Place in Denver, Colorado, the Denver Club was an opulent structure where Colorado's wealthiest men came to relax and broker business deals. Hawthbaren wore a blue silk smoking jacket, signifying that he was done with business for the balance of the day. He eased a cigar out of a cedar box, situated on a side table, and then unfolded a copy of the Rocky Mountain News dated Monday, October 6, 1900. Thumbing to the sports section, he glanced at a headline promoting the upcoming prize fight between Kid Parker and Joe Gans to take place at the Denver Athletic Club.

"Billy Edwards (Kid's Trainer) Will Have the Kid Ready to Fight" was the headline, and he pondered a potential wager while thinking that the current day boxers had gone soft since the bare-knuckle days of John L. Sullivan and James J. Corbett. Taking a puff off his Cuban cigar, Hawthbaren noticed his fellow club member Henry Wolcott approaching from across the room.

"Henry, have you received any correspondence from Vardon or his handlers regarding our proposal?" Hawthbaren asked as he lowered the paper into his lap.

Wolcott was the assistant manager of the Boston and Colorado Smelting Works, a Colorado state senator, and the owner of the Overland Park Country Club. Noticing the unfolded paper in Hawthbaren's lap, Wolcott advised,

"Put your money on the Kid, and as for Vardon, I received a telegram from his brother Tom confirming that he will be arriving in Denver next week, upon completion of his stay in Chicago following his US Open victory at the Chicago Golf Club this past weekend."

Hawthbaren nodded with satisfaction and invited Wolcott to join him for a drink. He ordered brandies from a young waiter, whom the members affectionately referred to as Sparky. With disheveled red hair, freckles, and a gap between his front two teeth, Sparky was a dead ringer for Huckleberry Finn. What members didn't know about Sparky was his affinity for gulping down the remains of unfinished cocktails. On many an evening, Sparky got drunk, right along with the membership.

"Do you find it surprising that Vardon would reach out to us and schedule a golf exhibition here in Denver? Overland Country Club is the only course here in Denver and a nine-hole one at that," Hawthbaren questioned, while glancing at his gold pocket watch.

"Maybe it's the $500 he will be paid to promote the Vardon Flyer golf ball in Denver and Colorado Springs the following week?" Wolcott replied.

"There is that; however, I feel as if there may be something else about our fair city that Mr. Vardon finds alluring. Do you have Vardon's exhibition match opponents lined up?" Hawthbaren questioned through the cigar smoke rising from his cigar.

"Indeed, I do; Vardon will play an eighteen-hole match against Overland Country Club Professional John Russell, our club's own Frank Woodward, and Mr. Walter Fairbanks, who recently immigrated here from Europe and has established himself as one of the finest amateur golfers in the area."

"Fairbanks? Isn't he the left-handed golfer who won a $200 bet at the Denver Athletic Club by swimming two lengths of the club's swimming pool underwater with but a single breath, while his legs were bound, and his hands tied behind his back?"

"It's not the first time he's picked wealthy pockets by performing that stunt," Wolcott answered while keeping a wary eye on Sparky, who was clearing the dishes from a nearby table.

The two men were about to transition into a conversation over the merits of the Philippine-American War when Hawthbaren's beautiful twenty-five-year-old daughter, Camille, entered the room. She spotted the two men and, after a brief hesitation, continued toward their table. She walked with an overt confidence, accentuated by both her stylishly tailored dark suit and youthful curves. Her chestnut hair was pinned up, and her olive skin was the perfect canvas for her emerald-green eyes. The old guard of men in the room looked on with envy as green as Camile's eyes as she passed by en route to her father's table.

"Young lady, you know you're not allowed in the men's Trophy Room!" Hawthbaren lovingly admonished.

"I do apologize for trespassing into this bastion of male dominance," she said, waving away the cigar smoke tickling at her nose. She bent down and kissed her father on the cheek. "My goodness, couldn't you powerful businessmen manage to open a window to let in some fresh air? It looks as if you're trying to communicate to each other via smoke signals!"

The two men raised their eyebrows at her irreverence, yet they couldn't resist smiling at the rush of femininity she interjected into the room.

"You remember my associate Mr. Wolcott, do you not?"

She nodded tepidly in Wolcott's direction.

"It's a pleasure to see you again, Miss Hawthbaren," Wolcott said, taking a hard look at the chewed end of his cigar.

"Father, I have some rather exciting news that, if not shared, will burst this medieval corset Mother insists I wear!"

CHAPTER TWO
THE JOURNAL
London, England, November 8, 1888

It was midevening in East London, and the damp, chilly air forced Londoners to seek comfort inside the Ten Bells Pub, located in the Whitechapel district of London. Sitting at a corner table of the pub was a well-built man of thirty years of age. His raven black hair was combed straight back over his scalp, and his facial features were handsomely arranged yet cast an impression of arrogance. He wore thick reading spectacles as a ruse, given that his eyesight was more than adequate. His overcoat, still moist from the elements, hung limp over an adjacent chair. He sipped English whiskey with an air of detachment while jotting down notes in a black journal. Notes that tried to explain terrible compulsions that had come over the man in the last six months and the horrible consequences of acting upon them.

Across the room from the man making notations in the journal, Charlie Swafford and Phillip Andersen stood at the bar, drawing on their pints of ale. Swafford, who had turned nineteen just the day before, was a young business student at the University of London. His boyish charm and quick smile endeared him to his fellow students, complete strangers, and the young ladies of London. The subject matter of their conversation at the bar jumped around like the toads croaking away in nearby Hyde's Park.

"I'll bet you a bottle of scotch that America will produce great golfers who will someday win our own Open championship. It's not in their nature to play second fiddle to us boys across the pond," Charlie challenged his friend.

"I don't see the game of golf catching on in America, old chap. The Yanks are much too practical to waste their time thrashing a ball around in a bloody field," Andersen countered, while keeping his eye on a group of young women on the other side of the establishment who were celebrating being released from their daily garment factory toils. The women, who were drinking ginger beer and waiting for the polka music to start up, invited looks of disapproval from the older patrons, whose days of spontaneous fun had long passed.

The man at the table, who was busy scribbling notes in the journal, was soon interrupted by a baby-faced sailor with curly blond locks.

"Hey, mate," the sailor slurred while steadying himself with an unsteady hand resting on the edge of the man's table. "Me name's Conrad, and I'm damn sure I saw you perform in the bloody circus a few years ago in maybe, Wembley, or Straford? I am a blooming bugger, but me memory is sharp as a cat's claw. Your name is Sam something?"

"Young man, you've got me confused with someone else. Now do yourself a favor and take your leave," replied the man at the table, backing it up with a look of contempt.

"No, no, come now, mate; I'm sure of it. Let me buy you a pint!" The sailor next attempted to pull over a splintered chair to join the man; however, his overture was scuttled like a sinking ship as the man at the table snatched the sailor's wrist and, in one powerful motion, sent him sprawling across the top of a nearby table, sending mugs crashing to the floor and splashing beer suds all over several burly longshoremen. Before a melee could ensue, two off-duty Whitechapel metropolitan police officers seated at a nearby table, discussing the grizzly unsolved Whitechapel murders, blew their whistles and quickly restored order. The man who had vanquished the sailor snatched up his coat and hurried out the door, forgetting the black journal, which had tumbled to the floor in the confusion.

Swafford and Andersen watched with amusement as the tall policeman sporting a bushy blond moustache was cheered like a local sports hero when he demanded new pints be brought over for the longshoremen. Swafford noticed the journal on the floor by the table. Feeling a sense of duty, he hurried over to retrieve it.

"Let's have a look," Andersen requested, reaching out his hand.

Swafford was about to relinquish the journal when they were interrupted by a factory girl with curly brown hair and milk-cow brown eyes.

"You boys look like you could dance a proper jig. The girls I'm with sent me over to inquire if you two gents are willing to be our dance partners for the evening?"

"What a shame. My friend here has to take his leave soon to attend to his university studies; however, I, Phillip Andersen, am at your beckon call for the evening."

"It's a shame your mate is so conscientious as he looks sweeter than plum pudding, but you'll do just fine," was her response before she hurried back to deliver the news.

Swafford pondered the journal, and decided the best course of action was to turn it over to the proprietor of the establishment. He caught sight of the bartender, who was returning back behind the bar after scolding one of the garment workers for using foul language.

"Excuse me, kind sir, I found this journal on the floor; perhaps the gentleman who left it will return to claim it."

"You can keep the damn thing!" the big, gray-bearded Irishman roared over the drone of German polka music that had just commenced. "I'm tired of babysitting all the rubbish you blokes leave behind!" he scolded, before turning his attention to a tub of soapy water and bobbing beer mugs. Tucking the journal inside his coat, Charlie waved goodbye to Andersen, who was now awkwardly juggling peanuts in front of a group of admiring ladies, and exited into the blackness of London.

Swafford was a hundred yards down Chelsea Street, nearing his flat, when he caught sight of a fast-approaching figure emerging out of the fog, heading in the opposite direction. The man was intent on his business and kept his head down as if the cobblestones under his feet were adding encouragement. There was no recognition for either man, yet, as fate would have it, the two would be sharing a cup of tea before night's end.

The man who crossed paths with Swafford continued on his way until, by chance, he stumbled upon Conrad, the sailor who had recognized him in the pub. He was crouched near a protruding finger of the Thames River, trying to rescue a cat that was clinging precariously to a half-submerged tree that was bobbing in the surging water. The man pulled his dagger, but the sound of the cat's distress softened his heart, so he hurried on to the Ten Bells Pub to gain back the procession of the precious journal with its diabolical secrets.

Upon entering the pub, he hurried over to the corner table where the earlier disturbance had occurred, only to find it occupied by an older gentleman with a weather-beaten face and yellowed teeth, chatting gaily with a middle-aged woman wearing a revealing black dress. Her plump face was smudged with mascara, and she leaned forward as if he were spoon feeding her.

"Good evening, sir, and madam; did you by chance find a black journal at this table? I left it here not long ago, and it is of the upmost urgency that I retrieve it."

"Haven't seen your bloody journal," replied the woman in a cockney accent. "So I would suggest you go poke your nose in someone else's business!"

"My apologies, as I see that you are peddling your wares." The woman's companion began to rise, however discretion prevailed and, he sat meekly back down, and resigned his interest to a bowl of half-eaten pretzels. "I'll let you two enjoy each other's considerable charms," he said, tipping his cap and making his way over to the bartender, who was in the middle of tapping a keg of beer that had been rolled out to meet the demand of the thirsty polka dancers. He quickly explained the situation of the journal to the frazzled bartender.

"A young gentleman did find it," he said, straightening up and stretching his sore back. "I told him to keep it as I'm not running a bloody pawn shop."

"You fool! Why didn't you secure it from him?"

"Sir, your bloody journal is no concern of mine. Now take your leave before I call a constable. I've had enough commotion in this place for one night." He snorted, turning his attention back to the white foam bubbling forth from the beer keg.

"I know the bloke who has your journal. He's a friend of mine by the name of Charlie Swafford," Andersen said, setting an empty beer mug on the bar top.

"Excellent, young man, it is very important that I gain possession of that journal!" He pulled two quid from his breast pocket and deposited them on the bar top, much to the delight of a tipsy factory girl who was clutching Andersen's arm for balance.

Charlie arrived back at his flat sometime after eleven o'clock in the evening. The dampness of the evening permeated his outer garments, and a shiver rattled his bones. He lit a kerosene lantern sitting atop a wooden table. After starting a fire in the hearth, he removed his overcoat and shook the raindrops free. He then set the journal on the table near the lantern. Dreading the school research paper, he put a kettle on the stove for tea, and returning to the table, he turned up the light from the lantern, which cast a glow on the walls, which Charlie normally found comforting, yet this evening found foreboding. He flipped the journal open, thinking that he might find some identification. At the top of the first page was the date of September 1, 1888. Below that was written, "What I did to Mary Ann Nichols." Just as his eyes focused on the narrative written below the name, he was interrupted by the heavy rapping of knuckles on the other side of his door.

CHAPTER THREE
SUFFRAGE

Denver, Colorado, October 6, 1900
Back at the Denver Club

"Father, I've been invited to join the National Women's Suffrage movement!" Camille announced. "It's been seven years since Colorado gave women the right to vote, yet unfortunately our voices have fallen on deaf ears in Congress." The excitement in her voice attracted a collection of furrowed brows that appeared over the tops of their playing cards. "I want to help gain suffrage rights for all women," she said, crossing her arms emphatically.

"Women should not be involved in politics, sweetheart. We've had this discussion before. Leave the dirty world of politics and business to men and concentrate on more worthy causes like raising a family and teaching our children," her father implored, looking in Wolcott's direction in a solicitation of support.

"I agree with you, Reginald," Wolcott chimed in. "In fact, I recently read that women can now get a driver's license in some states. That's plenty of equality for me!" he said, tapping the ashes from his cigar into the ashtray with a measure of satisfaction.

"Times are changing, Father. Those platitudes no longer define women. We shouldn't be pigeonholed into those narrow, traditional roles. It is my belief that women can perform any profession that men do, given the opportunity! And yes, we are quite capable of driving a car," she said icily, glancing in Wolcott's direction.

Hawthbaren raised his eyes to the ceiling in frustration, then waved Sparky over to the table.

"Sparky, be so kind as to bring my daughter a sarsaparilla?"

"Make that a scotch!" Camille corrected.

"Why do women want to be more like men? Next thing you know, they will be divorcing their husbands, going off to war, and sleeping with whomever they please!" Wolcott added, stamping out his cigar in the ashtray and pulling the newspaper over into his lap with aggression.

"Some men just can't see past their own noses!" Camille countered with finality.

Satisfied that she had made her point, she told her father that she'd see him at home for dinner later that evening, and made her way toward the door. Halfway there she intercepted Sparky, who was returning to the table with her scotch and soda. Camille hoisted the drink off the tray and, in a grand gesture, took a sip. The effect of the drink quickly registered a look of disgust, so she returned the unfinished drink to the tray and continued on her way, much to the delight of Sparky.

CHAPTER FOUR
THE BREAKUP
Denver, Colorado, October 6, Later That Evening

Camille entered the J.S. Appel clothing store on Sixteenth Street in downtown Denver. She had business to conclude, which did not include the purchase of any new fashions. In the morning she would be joining her mother and father on a weekend hunting trip to Estes Park, ninety miles northwest of Denver. They would be staying at the Estes Park Hotel as guests of western artist Albert Bierstadt, who with the help of his good friend Lord Dunraven, constructed the hotel in 1877. She walked by displays of the latest fur coats made of Persian lamb, mink, and chinchilla. Continuing through the store, she stopped at a rack of smartly displayed London topcoats. There, she encountered a full-length mirror and paused to take in her reflection, and thought, *You may not want to be dragged into the twentieth century Miss Hawthbaren, but the woman on this side of the mirror damn well won't be left behind!*

"My, how your reflection struggles to capture your beauty!" A familiar voice surmised from behind.

She turned to find Henry Wolcott leaning on his umbrella handle, sporting a look of amusement.

"Thank you for coming, Henry," she said, taking a step back from the mirror.

"Of course, my dear; however, this is not my idea of a romantic rendezvous," he said, fingering the lace of a dress hanging on a nearby rack.

"I apologize; however, the news I'm about to deliver could not wait."

"Really, I doubt if it could be more compelling than the news you delivered to your father and me at the club earlier today!"

"I've given our brief relationship a lot of thought, and I've decided to end it today. My father is becoming suspicious, and I don't see the point in it continuing now that I'm joining the suffrage movement and will be spending a considerable amount of time in Washington, DC."

"Miss Hawthbaren, darling, do I look like the type of man who gets pushed to the side by a mere child who has her head stuck in the clouds. This relationship ends when I'm good and, ready for it to end."

"Henry, you have a wife and two nearly grown children for god's sake; this isn't right for either of us!"

"I thought you wanted all the freedoms that men currently enjoy, including lying on your lovely back for anyone you damn well please," he chided.

"Henry, had I known you were so possessive, I would've never gotten involved!"

"So, you want to be treated like a man, my love?" He said, taking a menacing step toward her.

"I'll tell your wife!" She blurted, and with that he withdrew a step and rubbed his whiskers with the tips of his fingers. He fixed Camille with a look of anger, which quickly melted away into amused annoyance.

"You'll learn that love is not all peaches, and cream my dear!" Twirling his umbrella he briskly turned and walked back down the store aisle and back out onto the bustling streets of Denver.

CHAPTER FIVE
TEA FOR TWO

London, England, November 8, 1888
at Charlie's Flat

Annoyed by the hour of the intrusion and thinking the knocking might disrupt his neighbors, Charlie rushed to the door. Opening it brought him face-to-face with the mysterious man who had lost possession of the journal.

"The name is Doctor Thomas Reed, and I'm here to retrieve a journal that I inadvertently left at the Ten Bells Pub earlier this evening."

"Charlie Swafford at your service. My word, how did you find me?" Charlie asked.

"Your acquaintance, a Mr. Andersen, provided me with your whereabouts." Reed quickly sized up Charlie as a likeable, young man not prone to confrontation. Charlie stepped aside in a friendly manner to let the man enter.

"The journal is over on the table. Would you like a spot of tea to ward off the cold?"

"A cup of tea would indeed brace me for my return trip," he responded, thinking, *The tea will allow me time to ascertain exactly what my host knows about the contents of the journal.* He stepped into the room and brushed the raindrops from the sleeves of his topcoat.

"Please, hang your coat over a chair, and I'll prepare the tea." Charlie made his way over to the stove where he put the kettle on to boil.

Reed took a step closer to the table and noticed his journal was opened to the first entry about Mary Anne Nicholas. *Curiosity is the devil's breadcrumbs,* Reed thought to himself.

"Did you read the contents of the journal?" Reed asked, as he laid his wet coat over the back of one of the two wooden chairs at the table.

"Certainly not. I did, however, open it to ascertain any identification. Your knock on the door interrupted my inspection." Relieved, Reed reached across the table and greedily seized the journal. A few moments later, Charlie arrived back at the table with two steaming teacups. It was then that Reed noticed a worn canvas golf bag containing several rusted golf clubs leaning conspicuously up against the wall on the opposite side of the room. *A welcome distraction perhaps,* Reed thought, as he needed to decide what to do with the inquisitive student, who showed good taste in his recreational pursuits.

"I take it you're a fan of the game?" Reed asked, gesturing over to the golf bag.

"Indeed, I am! I was there to see Willie Park, Jr., win the Open Championship at Prestwick last summer. When my school year is complete in the spring, I hope to qualify for the British Amateur Championship at St. Andrews."

"By the way I did notice the name of Mary Anne Nicoles on the first page of your journal. Isn't that the name of the woman who was killed so gruesomely this summer by the so-called Jack the Ripper?" Thinking quickly like a cat cornering a mouse, Reed replied

"Yes, you are correct; I'm a medical doctor and was treating Miss Nicoles prior to her death. That entry in the journal was made the day of her last office visit. I have similar entries for all my patients. It's lucky for you that you didn't keep up your inspection, as there are strict laws covering doctor patient confidentiality in this country!" Reed countered with indignation, now thinking, *young Charlie may not live to see his graduation day.*

"No, Doctor Reed, I can assure you I had no further inspection of your journal. With that, Reed continued on in a friendlier tone.

"I'm rather a fan of this capricious game of golf myself. I play every chance I get when my medical practice allows. I must say, however, that playing the game left-handed presents quite a challenge when looking to acquire a set of clubs. Tell me, what method of grip do you employ on the putter?"

Charlie reached into the bag and removed the putter.

"Do you mind if I stand behind you to get a better look at how your hands look on the club?"

"Please do. Notice how I use a split grip on the putter, which allows my right-hand full reign during the stroke."

Once behind Charlie, Reed removed his dagger that was concealed up his right sleeve and was about to raise it when another knock fell upon the door.

"My bloody word!" Swafford lamented as he laid the putter back up against the bag and made his way to the door. "Pardon the interruption," he called over his shoulder, as Reed stealthfully concealed the dagger back under his sleeve, as if he were performing a routine magic trick.

"It's Miss Peale, your landlady." Swafford opened the door to find his landlady standing before him in her accustomed stooped posture. She wore a frayed, food-stained robe, spotted with cigarette burns. Her gray hair sat squashed under a hairnet, and an unlit cigarette dangled from her thin, chapped lips. Her beady eyes scanned the room behind Swafford and catching sight of Dr. Reed, she glared in his direction.

Damn it to hell, I can't kill Swafford now that this old hag has seen me. This bloke has more lives than King Henry had wives! Reed thought to himself.

"I've come to tell you that there was a young lady and young gentleman who stopped by here earlier in the day looking for you." The cigarette bobbed up and down with each spoken word, a sight Charlie found most amusing.

"What's so blooming funny!" she demanded.

"I'm sorry, Miss Peale; it's been a bugger of a day," Charlie answered, looking back at his guest, who nodded affably in agreement, before fixing the landlady with a malevolent glare.

"Here's the bloody note she left for you. Now take it, so I can get back to me beauty sleep." She tilted her head sideways to get a better look at Reed, as Swafford took possession of the note. "And I don't like nonresidents being in my blooming building at all hours neither," she called over Swafford's shoulder before finally turning and shuffling off backdown the hallway, the robe dragging obediently in her wake.

"Excuse the interruption, Doctor Reed; Miss Peale can be a bit of a nuisance. Now, I believe I was showing you, my grip."

"Think nothing of it. Please take the time to read your note, as it could be of an urgent nature."

"Very well," Swafford said, unfolding the note and scanning across its contents.

"It's from my friend Mary Kelly," he said before reading the remainder of the note. After digesting its contents, he looked at Reed and explained that she had stopped by earlier with her nephew Harry Vardon who, at eighteen years of age, had already made quite an impression upon the local golf establishment. "It's a pity that I was not home at the time, as her nephew, young Harry, will be leaving tonight to head back to the Isle of Jersey." He continued on, explaining that Mary had invited him to visit her flat tomorrow for tea and discuss a small loan of money that he might be able to lend. "I'm sorry to say that will be impossible, as I will be toiling all day with that incessant term paper, mocking me from the table over there."

"Quite frankly, Mr. Reed, Mary has had a rough go of it. I met her at Ten Bells Pub, where after a brief conversation, she propositioned me for intimate services in exchange for money. It turns out Mary has been working the streets as a prostitute for some time."

"Is that so?" Reed responded while taking a practice putting stroke with Charlie's Old Tom Morris putter.

"How dreadful that she's succumbed to such a lifestyle, I'd like very much for our community outreach manager, Beth Hunt, to send your friend some inspirational literature about changing her life. We would just need Mary's address to get that sent to her in our next mailing." Reed said, as a compassionate look spread across his face and the compulsion took full control.

"That would be very kind of you, Mr. Reed; she resides at 13 Millers Court, Dorset Street, in Spitalfields. Shall I write that down for you?"

"Not necessary," he replied, smiling. "When it comes to women in need of my services, I have a very good memory."

CHAPTER SIX
POOR MARY

London, England, December 1887,
The Sad Life of Mary Jane Kelly

Mary Jane Kelly became a widow at the tender age of twenty-one when her then-husband Joe Davies was killed in a Welsh mining accident when a coworker lost control of a coal car and watched helplessly as it rambled back down the tracks and crushed the unsuspecting Davies. This misfortune brought on Mary's nervous breakdown, and she was admitted to a sanitorium for eight months in the town of Cardiff, Wales.

It was there that a man named Gordon Spears befriended Kelly, eventually talking her into earning quick money as a prostitute to pay off her husband's accumulated gambling debts. Having returned to London in 1887 at the age of twenty-six, she drank heavily and continued to occasionally sell her body to earn enough money to pay the rent on her flat at 13 Miller's Court.

Late in 1887 Mary was fishing a half-eaten bag of fish and chips out of a rubbish bin, when she heard a young man's voice behind her.

"Are you Mary Jane Kelly from Wales?"

"Who in bloody hell wants to know?" she asked, spinning around.

"I'm Harry Vardon, your nephew from the Isle of Jersey," said the young man of eighteen.

"I'll be a pickle, you don't say! Last time I saw you, you were trying to hit a golf ball with a club that was taller than yourself. How did you find me?"

"Your sister Susan wrote me."

"Well, that is just bonny! Good to see you again; you're not such a little toad anymore, are ya? How's your little brother, Tom, a-doing?"

For the next two hours, Mary and Harry sat at a table in the Ten Bells Pub, catching up on lost time. Harry told her that he and his brother wanted to escape the Bailiwick of Jersey and pursue their dreams of getting into professional golf. When Mary asked young Harry what it was that captivated him so about the game of golf, Harry told her that he became smitten with the game after reading the compelling story of Young Tom Morris and how he lost his newlywed wife along with his unborn son during acute labor complications. Harry recounted to Mary how Young Tom rushed home from playing in a golf match only to find the county doctor helplessly standing beside his lifeless son and wife. He told it with such emotion that Mary's eyes welled up with tears, and she leaned her chin down into the palm of her hands, overcome with empathy.

She told Harry about her late husband being killed in the Welsh mining accident and about her new friend Charlie Swafford, who saw her as a kindred spirit trying to navigate the squalls of life; however, she couldn't bring herself to confide that she had been working the streets in order to keep a roof over her head and food in her shrinking stomach.

CHAPTER SEVEN
BLOODY MARY
London, England, Night of November 9, 1888

Mary Jane Kelly was home, alone finishing the book, Moby Dick. She identified with the life-and-death struggle between Captain Ahab and the whale. She had just come to the part where the whale is harpooned by Ahab, when a knock at the door dragged her eyes from the page. She hoped that it was Charlie Swafford, as in her note of the previous day, she had invited him to pay her a visit to chat over a cup of tea. She hurried over to the door, put her hand on the doorknob, and spoke through the faded wood.

"Is that you, Charlie?"

"No, Miss Kelly, the name is Doctor Thomas Reed, and I've been sent by our mutual acquaintance, Charlie Swafford."

Adjusting the ragged shawl that covered her shoulders, she asked, "Why would Charlie send you to visit me?"

"He's been called away on urgent family matters, and he wanted me to deliver to you some money, which he has gone to great lengths to secure. In fact, I was with Charlie in his flat yesterday when his land-lady delivered the note you left for him." The proposition of money, which would tide her over until she could find proper employment, was nibbling away at her caution like a rat on a sugar cube.

"If you were in Charlie's flat, Mr. Reed, tell me, what does he have standing over in the corner?"

"Why golf clubs, of course, Miss Kelly. It's his favorite pastime. It's frightfully cold out. May I come in and chase away the chill before satisfying all your questions?"

Mary Jane Kelly opened the door a crack and peered out. On the other side, she found a man of perhaps thirty, with a sturdy boxer's physique, holding his bowler to his chest in such a respectful manner that her last bit of trepidation melted away.

"I'm sorry. Any friend of Charlie's is allowed in my house," she said, stepping aside and allowing the stranger to enter.

As the uninvited guest was manipulating his way into Mary Kelly's flat, Charlie Swafford was in fact not away on business but rather signing his name to his finished term paper, "Business Practices for a New Age," which he had been working on all day and into the night. The paper would be late; however, the professor had taken a liking to young Swafford and would likely afford a measure of leeway.

Doing what he often did to clear his mind, he got up from the table and made his way over to the golf bag, where he removed the niblick and began making some practice swings, taking great care not to scrape the ceiling on his backswing and inviting the wrath of Miss Peele. The act of swinging the golf club cleared the cobwebs from Charlie's memory. Replacing the club in the bag, he walked over to a stack of London Times newspapers that were accumulating near the rubbish bin. He shuffled through them until he came upon the September 1, 1888, edition. On the first page, near the bottom, he found what he was looking for. "Woman Found Brutally Murdered in Bucks Row Identified."

Scanning the article, Swafford's eyes paused when he came to the sentence, "The victim's body, which was discovered the night of August

31, has been identified as Mary Anne Nicoles of 18 Thrawl Street." Thinking back on this visit of Dr. Reed the previous night, he remembered Reed saying the journal entry dated September 1 was the day he last saw Miss Nicoles, yet how could that be, when she was murdered on August 31? He decided that in the morning he would indeed accept Mary Jane Kelly's invitation and pay her a visit to check on her safety.

"Thank you, Doctor Reed, for dropping this money off from Charlie; he's such a peach!"

"Of course, Mary, it's my experience that everyone needs assistance from time to time."

"That's very kind of you, and I don't mean to be inhospitable; however would you be so kind as to leave the money and take your leave, as I have much to do this evening."

Reed was not interested in Mary's timetable and leisurely removed his topcoat and sat down on the only chair in the room, situated next to an old, rickety, three-legged table. He reached into the inside pocket of his topcoat and removed an envelope, placing it on the table. Mary moved closer and, uncrossing her arms, reached for the envelope only to have it snatched away by her guest. The ugly gesture sent Mary back a step, and her eyes widened with surprise.

"Mary is such a lovely name. Did I mention that my mother's name was Mary? She tried to raise a good boy, but sad to say she must be rolling over in her grave like a worm in manure. Why do women like you make me so angry, Mary?"

Mary had been hardened by the tough streets of London and would not be easily intimidated.

"Are you daft? My neighbor Joe Callas is a former constable, and I know for a fact he's residing on the other side of this bloody wall. If you don't leave now, I'll let out a shriek that can be heard in Liverpool!"

"Mary, I'm very particular about my business, so I took the liberty of sending your neighbor Mr. Callas on an errand. Funny what people will do for a few shillings? By the time the former constable arrives back, our business will have been concluded."

"What in bloody bollocks do you want, and why are you giving me money? This is the last time I'll ask—take your leave!"

"Mary, don't be a silly maid. This money isn't for you, as you'll soon have no need. It's for young master Harry Vardon. Charlie told me all about him, and I hope this money helps in his pursuit of the game of golf. Inside the envelope is a note I took the liberty of forging in your name. It will instruct the authorities to deliver the money to your nephew. Now isn't that a cracker of a plan, Mary?"

"Are you insane? Why wouldn't I just give him the money?"

"Because Mary, I'm going to be operating on you tonight to remove this affliction you carry. You may think that you are getting better; however, just like my poor mum, once a whore, well you know how the saying goes." With that he reached down to his right pant leg and carefully removed a serrated six-inch carving knife.

"Oh, Mother of Jesus, you're him," she whispered through trembling lips.

"They call me Jack the Ripper, but I think that's too unkind of a term for someone who is providing such a needed public service. Are you ready?" Reed asked, taking his finger, and running it along the length of the blade.

Mary Kelly reached over, removed her rosery beads off the headboard, and walked over to her guest.

"Be merciful and allow a condemned soul some mercy." She requested that he clasp them around her neck. He set the knife down to assist, and she sprang at him in an attempt to gain procession of the knife. He easily fended off her foray, and when she tried to scream, he covered her mouth and, in one quick motion, snapped her neck. He laid her body on the bed, rolled up his sleeves, positioned the knife and like any good doctor, got down to healing the afflicted. His fifth such operation in as many months. Business had indeed been good in London.

CHAPTER EIGHT
US OPEN CHAMPION
Chicago, IL, October 5, 1900
Before Traveling to Denver

Harry Vardon stood on the eighteenth tee of the Chicago Golf Club with one hole left to play in the 1900 US Open Golf Championship. He held on to a two-stroke advantage over his countryman, J. H. Taylor. As Vardon addressed the ball, he broke out in a cold sweat, gripped by a spasm of doubt that paralyzed him to such an extent that he was incapable of taking the club back away from the ball. Vardon's caddie, an English ex-professional strongman by the name of J. R. Cuddling, lowered Vardon's golf bag and stepped up next to him.

"Harry, I know what you're thinking. We will catch the bloody bastard this time, and let me assure you that your Aunt Mary Jane Kelly is resting in peace. In fact, I'm quite certain her spirit is amongst the gallery this very second, cheering you across the finish line. Now for God's sake, take the bull by the horns and knock the damn ball down the fairway so we can put a cherry on top of this championship and get us both a hot bath and a proper dinner!"

Cuddling's exhortation chased the fog from Vardon's head. Utilizing the effortless yet powerful swing that had captivated spectators all day, Vardon riffled his rubber core golf ball down the final fairway. "Now that's a ripper, Harry!" Cuddling yelled as he grabbed the club from Vardon and rumbled down the fairway in hot pursuit of the bouncing ball. *Damn, I wish he'd stop using that bloody term*, Vardon thought as he chased after his caddie's coattails.

After sinking the winning putt and hoisting the US Open trophy, Vardon spoke with several members of the assembled press. Soon after he and Cuddling relaxed on a bench near the clubhouse. Cuddling confirmed with Vardon that all the arrangements had been made for their exhibition match scheduled for the following weekend in Denver.

"Mr. Cuddling, take it upon yourself to secure lodgings at the Brown Palace Hotel in Denver and stay on full alert, as my instincts tell me that our man may be readying to strike again after all these years. I'll tie up the long-standing Buchannon case here in Chicago and meet you in Denver on Friday, October 10, two days before our exhibition."

"You can count on me, Inspector Vardon," Cuddling replied as he dutifully scraped mud from the bottom of the US Open champion and Scotland Yard detective's golf shoes with the tip of a small pencil that he'd been using to record scores on the champion's scorecard.

CHAPTER NINE
TEST OF STRENGTH
Denver, Colorado, October 8, 1900, Vardon's Caddie Arrives in Denver

The train from Omaha pulled into Denver's Union Station at 9:00 a.m. sharp. Passengers of all shapes and sizes disembarked under puffs of coal smoke that drifted above the train and disappeared into the backdrop of the Rocky Mountains. J. R. Cuddling may have been the most conspicuous of those departing the train as he stood five feet, eight inches tall, and weighed 250 pounds. His curly hair had thinned and was now flecked with gray. His dark brown eyes held remarkable vision for a man of forty, yet he wore glasses on occasion to project a greater air of sophistication. He had Vardon's golf bag slung over his shoulder and secured two suitcases with his free hands.

Once a professional strongman in England, Cuddling could do one-arm push-ups and tear the London phonebook in half with his bare hands. It was rumored that he quit the professional strongman business after being cheated out of several hundred pounds by his then manager Joey Higgins. After finding out about crooked dealings,

Cuddling hailed the first available carriage and made his way to Higgins's downtown London office. He confronted his arrogant manager over the faulty accounting, and when Higgins played dumb, Cuddling grabbed him by the ankles and dangled him out of the three-story window. He was pulled to safety only after agreeing to an accelerated repayment plan.

A weather beaten porter of African descent noticed Cuddling's predicament with the luggage and hurried over to assist.

"Can I give ya some hep, sir, with ya luggage there? Say what's in that strange satchel you got flung over ya shoulder, deh?"

"Indeed, my good man. The satchel you refer to is a golf bag. Are you not familiar with the game of golf?" he asked the porter, handing over the bags and sliding the golf bag off his thick shoulder to the ground.

"No, sir, never even heard of such a thing as golf. What y'all do with da funny sticks?" he asked.

"You take a ball and hit it into holes that are placed in a big field called a golf course. The game consists of getting the ball into eighteen of these holes in the fewest possible strokes."

"Sounds like a big waste of a fella's time, sir!"

This was an answer that Cuddling found quite amusing.

"There are indeed days that fit your assumption of the game, my good man," he replied, crossing his imposing arms.

"Okay, sir, maybe I'll hit that little ball me-self someday. Can I call ya a carriage?" Cuddling nodded and asked the porter if he was familiar with the Brown Palace Hotel.

"Yassir! Fanciest hotels dis-side of da Mississippi!"

The carriage arrived, but before climbing aboard, Cuddling bade farewell to the porter, giving him a silver dollar and a golf ball. The carriage quickly proceeded down Seventeenth Street to Tremont Place and the Brown Palace Hotel. Cuddling checked into room 613 where he unpacked, then gave Vardon's golf clubs a thorough scrubbing by holding the metal heads under water coming from the chrome faucet head hanging over the marble bathtub. Satisfied with the club's condition, Cuddling climbed into bed for a quick caddie nap.

Later that evening Cuddling got dressed in comfortably tailored, thirty-six-inch waist size trousers and an eighteen-inch neck size cotton dress shirt. Upon securing directions from the front desk, Cuddling walked out of the Brown Palace and briskly made his way up Tremont Street and over to the Denver Club, where he had a meeting scheduled for seven o'clock in the evening with the organizers of the upcoming exhibition match at the Overland Country Club.

Cuddling entered the Denver Club by strolling under the beautiful stone archway. Once inside he inquired of a gathering of gentlemen in the club's lobby as to the whereabouts of masters Henry Wolcott and Frank Woodward. They directed Cuddling to the billiards room located on the third floor. He tipped his cap and proceeded to the elevator where a man encumbered by having but one arm and dressed in a red bellhop uniform stood at attention. The poor fellow had lost his left arm repulsing a Spanish cavalry charge during the first weeks of the Spanish-American War.

"What floor, sir?"

When the elevator came to a stop three floors up, Cuddling gave the operator a generous tip and demonstrated an exercise the man could do with only one arm to keep himself in top shape.

"Might you be Mr. Wolcott and Mr. Woodward?" Cuddling inquired of two prominent-looking gentlemen seated in comfortable leather chairs snacking on buffalo chips, a signature snack of the club. The two men were dressed in tweed three-piece suites, discussing the pros and cons of the newly passed Erdman Act and how it might affect future railroad transportation costs.

"Yes, we are, and you must be Mr. Cuddling!" Wolcott replied as the two raised themselves from their chairs in a formal greeting.

"It's a pleasure to meet you gentlemen in your fair city of Denver," their visitor said, shaking hands.

"You must be quite fatigued after your long train ride out from Chicago; may I offer you a glass of cognac and toast your good friend and employer, Harry Vardon, on his US Open victory?" Woodward asked. He then offered Cuddling a fine Cuban cigar, which he normally reserved for his best clients at his downtown law practice, and motioned to Sparky to bring another glass of cognac for their guest. Cuddling ran the cigar under his nose and sat back, admiring the surroundings, which included the finest Italian furniture, billiard tables, and the most smartly dressed and finely groomed attendants.

"Gentlemen, you certainly have a handsome establishment here. It's a shame Harry could not be here with me to enjoy it, yet as you know from his brother's cable, he is concluding some business back in Chicago."

Sparky delivered the drinks and seemed to be on his best behavior as the three men toasted Vardon's good fortune at the US Open.

Wolcott went on to explain the format of the upcoming exhibition match at Overland. They would be playing an eighteen-hole match pitting the best ball score of Overland golf professional John Russell, Overland Country Club President, Frank Woodward, and a recently arrived English immigrant and fine amateur golfer, Walter Fairbanks, against Vardon's score. Wolcott described his Overland layout as a unique nine-holes laid out around the oval horse racing track.

"By chance is this Mr. Fairbanks also a member of this wonderful club?" Cuddling asked as he held a buffalo chip up to the light for closer inspection. Wolcott confirmed that although Fairbanks was indeed not a member of the Denver Club, he happened to be there that evening as a guest and was at that moment involved on the other side of the room in a high-stakes poker game. "Let us finish our discussion here, and then I'd like to meet this Mr. Fairbanks," Cuddling requested. *Luck, like a skunk, shows up when least expected*, Cuddling thought before biting down on a buffalo chip.

The three finished up their friendly banter with a story of how Cuddling and Vardon first became acquainted. Unbeknownst to them, they were both dating the same London actress, who went by the name of Patty Starr. They only found this out when she absentmindedly booked both on the same date. She only realized the oversight when she arrived at the rendezvous spot to find the two men sitting quizzically on the park bench next to each other, both with flowers in hand. She apologized profusely before mercifully breaking up with both men on the spot, stating that it was the only fair solution for all parties. After she made haste in departing the scene, the two men shared a hearty laugh at the absurdity of the situation and chatted for some time.

Getting on so well, the two men left the park, took a short walk over to the Fly on the Wall pub, and continued their conversation. There, Vardon explained his rather unique dual identity as both a professional golfer and a Scotland Yard detective. He explained to Cuddling the horrific killing of his aunt, Mary Jane Kelly, at the hands of Jack the Ripper and his obsession with trying to bring her killer to justice. The two were several pints in when Vardon made a proposal to his new friend.

"Mr. Cuddling, this proposition may sound preposterous as we have just become acquainted, but I'm looking for a partner."

"A partner, Mr. Vardon?"

"Indeed, Mr. Cuddling, I'm looking for someone to be a steady hand at my side on the golf course as I chase major championships as well as assist me in bringing fugitives of the law to justice, with the fiend Jack the Ripper being at the very top of our list."

"And how would I be compensated, Mr. Vardon, and please don't tell me by my good looks as I'd likely starve to death.?"

"You'll receive the handsome sum of one hundred dollars a week along with room and board."

"And what happens when we capture this jolly Jack the Ripper fellow?"

"Why, Mr. Cuddling, we will be the most famous crime fighters in the world!" And with that, Vardon wrote up the contract on a bar top napkin, and the two men shook hands. *I'd take a bullet in me willie-sack for this man, Cuddling thought, folding the napkin, and slipping it into coat pocket.*

Back at the Denver Club, the three men concluded their discussion and made their way over to the card table, where a pile of bills in front of Fairbanks advertised that he was profiting at the expense of less experienced gamblers. They stood a few yards away from Fairbanks's table; Woodward commented that not only was Fairbanks one of the finest amateur golfers in the state, but he also held several weightlifting records over at the Denver Athletic Club, where he was a member.

"You don't say. I know something about feats of strength myself, as I was a professional strongman in London some dozen years ago," Cuddling boasted. He went on to explain that he thought highly of his strongman abilities until he made the mistake of challenging the great Canadan strongman Louis Cyr, who was in London in 1893 putting on an exhibition. Cuddling deadlifted 450 pounds. Cyr slapped him on the back and boasted that he could lift 500 pounds off the ground with one finger. Skeptical onlookers stared in amazement when Cyr had the weights tied up with ropes with a loop made at the end to slip his index finger through. There were gasps of disbelief when the Canadian behemoth wasted little time in hoisting the bloody mass of iron several inches off the ground.

Woodward was aptly impressed by the story and asked Cuddling if he would not mind giving them a demonstration of his strength.

"Indeed, I'd be happy too as long as Mr. Fairbanks is a participant." With that they made their way to the table where Walter Fairbanks was shuffling the cards in preparation for another profitable poker deal.

"Walter, meet Mr. J. R. Cuddling from England. He's Harry Vardon's valet and trusted golf caddie. When I explained that not only would you be playing in the exhibition against Vardon but that you are also the strongest man at the Denver Athletic Club, he was keen on meeting you."

Woodward said, "Mr. Cuddling claims to have been a professional strongman back in England." Fairbanks raised an eyebrow at this revelation and casually stood while inserting his winnings into a shiny money clip.

"I'm not in the claiming business, Mr. Wolcott," Cuddling said, rolling up his sleeves.

Cuddling inherited his strength from both parents. His father was a burly Welsh miner, and his mother earned additional money for the family by frequenting the local Welsh pubs and challenging liquored up miners to arm wrestling matches.

"I also performed in a French traveling circus troupe back in London in the late eighties," Fairbanks pointed out in a tone that announced he was not about to take a back seat in the strength department to a mere caddie, no matter how robust in appearance. After a brief discussion, it was agreed that the fairest test of strength would be a seated, one-armed overhead press with a 150-pound dumbbell. Two busboys, who included Sparky, were dispatched to the gymnasium to retrieve the dumbbell, while Wolcott pulled over a sturdy wooden stool. The dumbbell was soon retrieved by the two huffing and puffing youngsters, each securing one end of the massive dumbbell. By this time there was a crowd of curious members and staff gathered around to watch the spectacle.

"Mr. Fairbanks, you have the honors," Wolcott said as he directed the positioning of the dumbbell next to the stool. Fairbanks sat on the stool, and after a couple of deep breaths, he hoisted up the dumbbell with both hands and settled it over his left shoulder, where after a momentary pause to balance the weight, he pressed it up to an extended position above his head. Encouraged by the claps and gasps of admiration, he performed another repetition before lowering it back to the ground with a satisfied grunt, and removing a handkerchief dabbed at the perspiration on his forehead.

"Walter, that was an impressive show of strength!" Woodward complimented. Fairbanks only nodded as he unrolled his sleeve and reclasped his cuff link. "Mr. Cuddling, we don't expect you to travel on a train all day and then come in here and do unreasonable stunts. Let's be prudent and call it an evening," Woodward proposed. A suggestion that quickly elicited boos from the spectators, who were placing bets, and drinking with renewed enthusiasm.

"I'll have nothing of the sort!" Cuddling responded, and after congratulating Fairbanks on his impressive mastery of the weight, Cuddling strolled over to the two young busboys, who were glued to the proceedings, and whispered something in their ears. Returning to the chair, Cuddling did not sit but rather lowered himself to the ground in a push-up position. "Okay, lads, I'm ready," and with that, the two boys hurried over and straddled Cuddling's back as if riding a bucking bronco.

Cuddling sat down on the stool and proceeded to raise the dumbbell with both hands and although he was right-handed, he settled the weight over his left shoulder, then pressed the weight over his head two repetitions, matching Fairbanks, before he lowered the weight back to earth with a resounding thud.

"Gentleman, I declare the competition a draw!" Woodward announced as the spectators mingled about. A few of the larger men sucked in their paunch and declared they too could master the weight. When Cuddling raised himself off the chair and reached for his coat, Fairbanks strolled over to offer his congratulations.

"Mr. Cuddling, you truly are a world-class strongman. May I have your autograph on the club's newsletter?" He set the newsletter down on a table next to his combatant.

Cuddling removed the same pencil from his shirt pocket that he'd used to mark Vardon's score card and signed the newsletter, setting both items back down on the table.

"Gentlemen, I look forward to our exhibition this week," Cuddling said, shaking hands with his guests, including Fairbanks, who appeared gracious yet eyed his fellow Englishman with suspicion as Cuddling made his way back out to the elevator. Once back down in the lobby, Cuddling requested that he be permitted to use the club's telephone to call Vardon at the Chicago Athletic Club where he was staying. After several rings the operator picked up the line and transferred the call to Vardon's room.

"Hello, Harry, how're your business prospects looking in Chicago?"

"Mr. Cuddling, I'm glad you found your way to Denver. For my last meeting tomorrow, I'll be wearing my detective hat as I address the smoldering situation with the president of the American Tobacco Company. Tell me old boy have you located the whereabouts of a certain Walter Fairbanks?"

"I have Harry, and I must say, if he's a wolf in sheep's clothing, he wears them rather well."

CHAPTER TEN
FARMER'S DAUGHTER
Greeley, Colorado, October 6, 1900,
A New Start from an Unlikely Source

Claire Davis couldn't stomach life on the family farm outside of Greeley, Colorado, any longer. When she turned sixteen years old, her father tried to molest her in the barn as she was milking the family cow.

Before sunrise the following day, Claire packed a small bag of clothes and crept to the edge of the farm, where after looking back with tear-filled eyes, she bolted along the railroad tracks south. She left a note for her mother, telling her she loved her and that she wanted a different life than what they could offer her on the farm. She left her father a note apologizing for the five dollars she took from the family till and warning that if he ever tried to bring her back to the farm, she'd either stab him, or herself.

After two days of walking, Claire found herself in Denver, where after some searching, she found the cheapest, most run-down hotel in Denver. The next day, unable to find work in the shops and small businesses, Claire spied an advertisement on the very back page of the Denver Post for "Lady Entertainers." She summoned her courage, and stepping over a sleeping vagrant in the alley, she made her way to the location referenced in the paper.

She ended up at the High Peaks Saloon, located on Market Street in Denver. The saloon served as a front for the Fallen Angel Bordello. Searching for a friendly face, all she managed to find was a scruffy looking bartender, who was rolling a cigarette on the bar top. She informed him that she was responding to the advertisement in the paper. Without looking up, he asked her how old she was. When she lied and said eighteen, he pointed a crooked index finger as if it were a six-shooter in the direction of a door at the back of the saloon with a sign hanging on it that read, "Knock Before Entering." Claire made her way over to the door and timidly tapped three times.

"Who is it?" a woman's gravelly voice boomed from the other side of the door.

"The name's Claire Davis, and I'm responding to the advertisement in the paper."

"In that case, sweetie, come in and let me have a look at you!" *I'm in desperate need of a girl to work the late-night shift*, the woman behind the door thought to herself. Claire turned the handle on that door and pushed it open to find Mattie Silks, the madam of the Fallen Angel Bordello, slumped behind a large mahogany desk, playing solitaire. Her only company being a whiskey bottle and a smoldering cigar in the ashtray. She stared hard at Claire and saw right away the potential of the skinny redhead with honey-colored skin and pale blue eyes. "Darling, I need a girl to start work tonight. Might that girl be standing right here in front of me looking so pretty?"

Later that evening Claire stood over in the corner of the High Peaks Saloon dressed in a frilly barmaid's costume and wondered if she would have the nerve to fulfill her required job duties. She was contemplating an attempt to sneak out the back door when a newcomer to the establishment wondered in from the street. He wore a brown suit with a matching vest and took a table near the back of the room.

He ordered a glass of whiskey from the same bartender with the trigger-happy finger. When the drink arrived, he opened a journal and, removing a small pencil from his breast pocket, wrote the date at the top of the first page while fighting the urge to itch at the fake mustache he hid behind. He then wrote the following: *I've been sent to this place by the same compulsion that directed my misdoings in London twelve years earlier. Who the poor soul is that will reap my madness I do not know.*

"Hello, my name is Claire. Are you looking for some company tonight?" she asked interrupting his notations. She stood awkwardly at his table, while wondering if she looked as ridiculous as she felt.

"You look like a lost kitten," he finally replied, as he took a sip of whiskey and looked at her through a veil of amusement.

"I like a man with an accent! Are you a writer?" she asked, pointing down at the journal.

"My personal business is not something I'd like to share, nor is it something you'd wish to hear," he replied. "Tell me, why would a nice girl like yourself work in an establishment such as this?"

"To be honest, I'm just a hungry sixteen-year-old farm girl who ran away from home this week after my father tried to molest me." She plopped down exhausted, on the other chair at the table and exhaled, which loosened one of her reddish curls, causing it to fall across her long, straight nose. The sight not only amused the man, but it thawed a heart that had come to accustomed to rage of not his own making.

"So, you just started this work and have never been with a man?"

"This is my first night, and you're in line to be my first customer. I hope you don't mind that if we do go upstairs, I have to charge you more on account of the virgin fee," she informed. The man at the table laughed heartily at that, but before he could reply they were interrupted by the bartender, who wandered over to check on Claire.

"Claire, you need to move along from this fancy dandy here and start earning your keep."

"She's with me," the man at the table replied calmly. "Now go back behind the bar where you belong. If you want to make yourself useful, bring us two meals of steak and potatoes along with two cold beers."

Claire's mouth watered at the mere mention of the food.

"What did you just say?"

"You heard me, unless you're both deaf and dumb," the man at the table replied.

The bartender had thrown many a drunken patron out the door before, yet he sensed the man with Claire could be dangerous, so he decided to defer the prickly situation over to Maggie's professional bodyguards.

"If you're not moving towards the door by the time I get back to the bar, limey, there's going to be pain and suffering coming your way," he said, flashing Claire a malevolent smile and making his way back over to the bar.

"Listen, mister, I don't want me no trouble with Miss Mattie!" Claire said, keeping her eye on the bartender, who was now behind the bar talking to a big, black-bearded, bald man who had a nasty looking disposition.

"Who in bloody hell is this, Mattie, that you speak of?"

"Please don't tell her I said anything! I'm supposed to take three customers upstairs this evening, charging the first fella twenty dollars for the virgin fee; that would've been you."

"Yes, I gathered," he replied.

"Then two more gents at ten dollars each, for a total of three customers a night. Then, after handing over the money to Mattie at the end of the night, I would be paid five dollars, along with a meal back in the kitchen and a room to sleep in with another girl named Goldie. She gave me these," she said, pulling three rubbers from the costume pocket and exhaling air that again ruffled the red curls hanging across her forehead.

"I will have a chat with this Mattie woman later this evening, but for now, Claire, this is your first and last night working in this sewer hole." He removed twenty dollars from his trouser pocket and replaced the rubbers in her hand with the money. He threw the rubbers back over his should and one of them landed in the bowl of soup of a surprised customer.

"For now, get yourself a room at the Brown Derby Hotel down the street and wait for me to contact you again. Register under Miss Polly McFarland and stay locked up in your room until I arrive to check on you. Claire, would you be willing to leave Denver with me?"

"I do, I will, I mean, I am," she said, frazzled to the point of not caring anymore.

"For our purposes my name is Doctor George. Now go ahead and take your leave, Claire."

The huge bald man with the black beard, along with a smaller, yet no less sinister-looking man with a ponytail and a limp to his gait, strolled over to the table. Before a single word was exchanged, several adjacent tables cleared of their occupants as if two rats had just crawled on scene.

"Claire, get yar lazy arse up and go see Mattie. She's waiting for you in the office!" the bearded giant ordered through broken teeth, his words accompanied by a slight whistling sound.

"Claire, do as I instructed." The man at the table encouraged.

She froze with fear, not knowing what to do.

"Trust me, Claire, now go!"

She hurried out the front entrance onto Larimer Street. Once outside she made her way over to a carriage horse that stood motionless, breathing puffs of steam into the night air. She stroked the horse along the length of its nose and asked, "When did you make it off the farm, lovely lady?"

"Gentlemen, as of now, Claire has officially retired from the entertainment business."

"We don't take orders from riffrafts, who wander in off the street. Juno, you go out and rustle up that little bitch and take her to Mattie's office before she gets us both canned!" Blackbeard ordered.

The man with the limp moved toward the outside door but never made it, as the man at the table rose and, seizing Juno's ponytail, yanked him back so hard that his head bounced off the side of the table with a sickening thud, knocking him out stone-cold. Blackbeard pulled a knife and lunged at their assailant, but his intended target sidestepped the charge with the agility of a big cat and landed a perfectly timed punch to the man's side, rupturing his spleen. Blackbeard dropped to the floor, like a load of dirty laundry immobilized by the pain. Claire's protector then pulled out his own knife and slit the man's Achilles tendons, causing a queer popping sound that no one within earshot would soon forget.

CHAPTER ELEVEN
MATTIE GETS A VISITOR
Downtown Denver, Colorado, October 9, 1900

Later that evening Mattie Silks stood at the bar of the High Peaks Saloon, questioning Juno.

"Why am I paying you and Rosco if you can't protect my girls from the scrabble that wander in off the street?"

"I got jumped from behind by that son of a bitch," he said, rubbing the lump on the back of his head. "How's Roscoe doing? I heard he got worked over pretty good by the Englishman."

"He's recovering in the hospital, and he won't be any good to me once he gets out. I want you to find Claire Davis and bring her back to me. I better not find so much as a bruise on her body, or you'll be back washing dishes in the kitchen, understood?

"Yes, Miss Silks, don't worry. I'll track her down. What about the Englishman?"

"You'll get a big bonus if you can manage to kill that brute and make it look like a robbery."

"No worries—we'll take care of him," Juno said, raising a makeshift bag of ice to the back of his throbbing head.

"Don't let anyone disturb me; I got paperwork to finish," Silks ordered, grabbing a bottle of whiskey from behind the bar and making her way back into her office, locking the door behind her. Moving around her desk, she noticed that the window was partially open, yet she couldn't recall opening it earlier in the day. Closing the window, she sat at her desk, poured herself a drink, and commenced rolling a cigarette. *With the police in my back pocket and finding the final girl I need, things are too good to have some bleeding-heart Englishmen coming in off the street and shitting in my hat,* she thought to herself.

"So, you're the big shot, madam?" a voice questioned from behind her changing curtain. Silks was startled yet gained her composure by the time the man stepped from behind the curtain and took two strides toward her desk.

"And you must be the dumb-cluck Englishman who jumped my bodyguards. Where is Claire? I want her back here by tomorrow noon, as she will draw in customers quicker than you can say London Bridge is falling down. You must be mighty full of yourself to think you can cross old Mattie."

"Not only will Claire not be returning, but you'll release all of your girls and close down this bloody place. After all, I can't possibly kill all of them now, can I?" he said, peeling off his fake mustache and depositing it into the trash can next to Silks's desk.

Silks broke out in a belly laugh so hard that her eyes began to water.

"I must say, I appreciate your English wit, I haven't had this much fun since a girl of mine named Two-Ton-Tilly entertained our Chief of Police. Now, I wish I had more time to continue with our banter; however, I've got a business to run," she said, reaching into her desk drawer and extracting a Lugar pistol. "Now turn and put your hands against the wall."

He shrugged off the order, not too concerned with the gun being introduced into the equation. Silks reached under her desk and pushed a concealed button, which activated a buzzer in the bar to alert the bouncers that there was trouble in her office. When no one stirred outside her door, Silks cursed and pushed it again and again.

"Clever idea to have a warning buzzer concealed under your desk; however, I learned my lesson many years ago in Paris when a similar device nearly did me in. Now, in regard to that Lugar of yours, I took the liberty of removing the bullets." Silks squeezed the trigger, only to be dismayed by the click of an empty chamber.

"Who the hell are you?" She demanded, seething.

"My line of work combines both saving lives, which I have control over, and murder which I don't. Unfortunately for you the ladder applies to our meeting today. You may be familiar with my murderous side as he ran rampant in London a dozen years ago."

"Enlighten me!" She fumed, throwing the empty revolver at the intruder's head, which he easily avoided. *I better think fast, as this devil has gained the upper hand*, she thought, moving around her desk, and approaching her adversary. "Just imagine a man of your talents and a woman with my business savvy could make a rather successful partnership. I give these women employment. If it weren't for me, they'd be out on the street begging for food." She moved closer still until she stood only a few inches from the man, her lips close enough that he could smell whiskey on her breath. She put one hand on his shoulder concealed in the other was a pocketknife that she raised in a slashing motion aimed at his throat.

He caught her wrist in midair, the blade inches from opening an artery. She struggled with the futility of a man trying to pry a banana from a gorilla. Holding her arm in place and complying with the compulsion that was now orchestrating his actions like a symphony conductor, bent down, and whispered in her ear, "Never kid a killer, especially when your killer is Jack the Ripper," and redirected the knife across her own throat, ending the reign of old Mattie Silks in Denver.

CHAPTER TWELVE
DINNER GUEST

Estes Park, Colorado, October 7, 1900

Camille Hawthbaren and her parents checked into adjoining rooms at the Estes Park Hotel, 8,000 feet above sea level in Estes Park, Colorado. After washing up the family met for an early dinner in the lodge's rustic dining room, which featured several big game heads mounted on the walls. Camille was dressed in a lovely green dress that accentuated her natural beauty. Her father wore a simple gray suit and black bow tie, and her mother wore a full-length wool dress. They sat at a table with a lovely view of Longs Peak in the distance.

Camille was still worried about the affair she had so foolishly engaged in with Henry Wolcott, yet the change in scenery and mountain air made her feel renewed and resilient again. In fact, she very much wanted to get her brief relationship with Wolcott out into the open so that it wouldn't follow her around like a lost cat.

"Father, I have something to tell you."

"I hope you have come to your senses about this suffrage movement nonsense," he responded, hoping to gain the upper hand on the presumed subject matter.

"Dear, I think Camille has every right to follow her conscience in the matter of women's equality," Camille's mother interjected while checking her makeup in a small pocket mirror.

"Darling, do you really want your daughter to be more like a man? Next thing you know, she'll be wearing pants, swearing like a sailor, and disobeying the wishes of her husband. Is it not too much to ask for a woman to know her place in this world?" Hawthbaren questioned as he moved on from the crab Louie to spreading butter vigorously on a dinner roll. The room, with its western artwork, polished wood furnishings, and hanging animal heads, seemed to back up Hawthbaren's assertion that it was indeed a male-dominated world.

"Father, once again you're missing the point. I don't want to live my life as a man. I want to keep my femininity, while also having equal opportunities for careers and social standing. Tell me, why don't you have a woman member at the Denver Club? Overland Country Club has women playing golf right along with the men."

"I told you, darling, we should not have let her go back east last summer to attend that women's retreat thing at Dartmouth College!" he said, continuing to take out his frustration on the innocent dinner roll.

"Equality Conference!" both Camille and her mother corrected in unison.

"Mother, that is priceless," Camille said, laughing into her napkin.

"Oh, my word, you two ladies are incorrigible," he said, waving over the waiter, who was occupied filling the water glasses at a nearby table and sending lovesick glances in Camille's direction.

"Waiter, would you be so kind as to bring to the table a bottle of your finest champagne, as we have some celebrating to do."

"Of course, sir, and are we celebrating a birthday this evening?" the waiter asked, looking hopefully in Camille's direction.

"Just bring the champagne if you don't mind."

This response hijacked the waiter's eyes away from his daughter and propelled him toward the kitchen. Hawthbaren broke some news of his own by explaining to his wife and daughter that his business associate Mr. Henry Wolcott had decided to give up his senate seat and run for governor and that he would like to have him on the ticket as lieutenant governor. This news nearly caused Camille to choke on a cracker.

"Reginald, this is the first time you've spoken of this," his wife said.

"Fellow members of the Denver Club have been pushing for a strong business leader to run as the Republican challenger to the Democratic incumbent, Charles Thomas, who seems more interested in getting people lynched than increasing business opportunity here in Denver."

"Father, how does Mr. Wolcott feel about strong labor unions, which protect workers on matters of working conditions, hours of work, and safety?" Camille challenged.

"Let's have peace at this table for the rest of the evening, shall we?" Hawthbaren's wife insisted as the waiter arrived at the table with the champagne and glasses. As the cork was being extracted from the champagne bottle, Hawthbaren announced that he would be joining his friend Albert Bierstadt on a big game hunting trip in the morning. He asked his daughter if she would like to come along on the hunt, as she was so interested in pursuing manly endeavors.

"I'll take no part in the wanton slaughter of innocent animals!" she said, while trying to dislodge another cracker from its wrapping.

"What would you like to do tomorrow?" her mother asked, accepting a half-full glass of champagne from her husband.

"Might I suggest playing some golf?" an English-accented voice asked from the table behind the Hawthbaren's. The gentleman had slipped into the room quite unnoticed. Camille swiveled in her chair.

"Good sir, your suggestion is wholly unsolicited," Hawthbaren barked while pouring a moderate amount of champagne into a glass intended for Camille.

"Father, why won't you fill Mother's and my champagne glasses? Are you afraid we will embarrass you with our drunken antics?" Camille asked.

The question elicited a grumbled response from her father. Camille's mother scolded her husband for being so standoffish and reminded him that they were indeed on vacation and in such a lovely place.

"Father often talks about golf, yet whenever he comes home from playing the silly game, he's in a dreadful mood. Does golf have a similar effect on you?" she asked the handsome stranger.

"Young man, if you intend to continue this conversation with my daughter, the least you can do is come over and make a proper introduction of yourself!"

The man dabbed at the corners of his mouth with the tip of his red napkin, then strolled over to the Hawthbaren's table. He was dressed in a comfortable pair of dark trousers and a gray cashmere sweater that struck Camille as the perfect mountain attire.

"Charlie Swafford, by way of London, England," he said, shaking hands with Hawthbaren and bowing slightly to the ladies at the table. Camille batted her eyes and swooned at Charlie, just to get a rise out of her father, which caused Camille's mother to swat at her daughter's hand with her napkin.

"My name is Reginald Hawthbaren, and this is my wife, Sarah, and my sometimes-incorrigible daughter, Camille. What business do you have here in our fair state of Colorado?"

Swafford went on to explain that he was in the employ of George B. Walker, the founder of the Locomobile Company of America and editor and publisher of *The Cosmopolitan* magazine. He was sent west to scout locations for a possible new automobile manufacturing facility.

"*The Cosmopolitan* magazine!" Camille gushed. "Mother, that's the magazine that sent Elizabeth Bisland on an around-the-world trip. They publish human interest stories along with serialized novels such as H. G. Wells's *War of the Worlds*."

"I'm sorry to inform you, Miss Hawthbaren, that I know little of that side of my employer's business. My expertise is in the promotion of automobile transportation."

Camille wrinkled her nose and dabbed her lips with her napkin in a show of disappointment.

"Very interesting, young man; you happen to be speaking with the president of Denver Tramway Company."

"Is that so, sir? I'm honored indeed!"

"Now, Father, before you get started on a droll conversation about the best way to move the masses, I'd like to accept Mr. Swafford's kind invitation to play golf."

"Before you begin the impossible task of trying to explain golf to my daughter, Mr. Swafford, are you aware that your countryman Harry Vardon will be giving an exhibition next week in Denver at the Overland Country Club?"

"You don't say! Mr. Vardon and I met twelve years ago after the passing of his aunt. I followed Mr. Vardon around Royal St. George's last year when he won his third Claret Jug. I'm similarly thrilled to read about his recent victory at the US Open in Chicago!"

"What's a Claret Jug?" asked Mrs. Hawthbaren, looking perplexed at her husband.

"Sounds like something you blow into on the back porch after too much elderberry wine," Camille answered. "I'm sure Mr. Swafford can enlighten us."

"The Claret Jug is what they give to the winner of the Open Championship," Charlie explained.

Mrs. Hawthbaren turned to her husband. "Perhaps you could invite Mr. Swafford down to Denver as our guest for the exhibition. Would that be okay with you, Camille?"

Camille raised her champagne glass.

CHAPTER THIRTEEN
GOLF LESSON

Estes Park, Colorado, October 8, 1900

Camille met Charlie for breakfast in the hotel's dining room at nine o'clock the next morning. She was outfitted in a loose-fitting, full-length skirt and a button-down tan blouse. Charlie was dressed in dark trousers with a white shirt, a red vest, and a black bow tie. Lying next to the table was Charlie's golf bag. *Don't we make a splendid couple?* Camille thought, and when the waiter asked if they were on their honeymoon, Camille blushed. They both ordered eggs Benedict, coffee, and fresh-squeezed orange juice.

"Mr. Swafford, do you always take your golf clubs with you wherever you go?"

"Please call me Charlie, and yes, why not? You never know when you'll meet a beautiful damsel in distress needing a golf lesson," he said, chuckling.

The waiter arrived with the breakfast tray. Both were famished, having stayed up late into the night listening to Hawthbaren's travel, golf, and hunting stories. It was only after Mr. Hawthbaren polished off the contents of the third bottle of champagne and began talking about his premarital romances that Camille's mother called a halt to the proceedings and ordered everyone to bed.

Camille requested the waiter bring them a newspaper, just as the food arrived.

"Are you like myself and revel in keeping up with current affairs?" Swafford asked as he ground a liberal amount of pepper over the hollandaise sauce, smothering his eggs.

Camille told Charlie that as a child, before she could go out and play in the evenings, her father insisted that she read the paper and summarize to him the events of the day. She also explained that her ambition was to someday become a writer for the *Rocky Mountain News*, covering the critical issues of the day, much like Nellie Bly did for the *Pittsburgh Dispatch*.

The waiter arrived back at the table with a newly arrived copy of the *Rocky Mountain News* and set it down with the front page facing Camille. There staring up at her was the face of Henry Wolcott, with the headline "Wolcott to Run for Governor." Taking a sip of coffee, Camille was relieved that she didn't divulge her affair with Wolcott. The fact that her father was now Wolcott's running mate for governor certainly complicated things. *My god, I wish I had exercised better judgment when it came to Henry's romantic advances*, she thought to herself, cutting into her eggs, and watching the yolk ooze without boundaries, much like how fate weaves its way through people's lives.

"Charlie, have you ever done something that was so utterly dim-witted that you wanted to throw yourself off a bridge and into an alligator-invested river?"

"Camille, if I may say so, I'm the king of dim-wittedness. I have a saying: It is better to err in judgment than to err against one's beliefs."

"I like that, Charlie; may I borrow it?"

"Yes, especially if it prevents you from sacrificing yourself to the alligators. Say, is that the friend of your father who's running for Governor?" Charles asked, pointing a finger at Wolcott's picture, and reaching for a warm corn muffin nestled in a basket at the center of the table.

"Yes, it is," she said, taking another sip of coffee. Her eyes then landed further down the page at another headline, "Madam Found Murdered in Denver Saloon." "Brutality against women needs to be an issue in the next election!" Camille said.

"Why do you say that?" he asked, pushing his plate away and dabbing his mouth with a napkin.

"I'm looking at an article on the front page about a madam of a brothel being stabbed to death." She pushed the paper away in disgust.

Charlie slid the paper over and scanned the article, which went on to describe the murder, including the way the victim's body was positioned with her arms folded across her chest.

Camille noticed the color had drained from his face. "What is it, Charlie? You've gone as white as the tablecloth!"

Swafford went on to explain the events of twelve years ago, starting with the journal and his encounter over tea with Jack the Ripper, culminating in the horrible death of his friend Mary Jane Kelly.

"Oh my god, Charlie, I have no words; what a horrific chain of events. We read about those horrible murders perpetrated by that fiend." She laid her hand lightly on top of his.

"I accept your father's invitation to attend the exhibition match next week. Now, wouldn't you say it's a lovely day for a game of golf?"

After breakfast Camille and Charlie freshened up and then met outside the hotel, where they took a short carriage ride over to the rudimentary nine-hole golf course laid out on property owned by the Elkhorn Lodge. Charlie set the golf bag down on the first tee box and proceeded to take a handful of dirt from a sandbox. He placed a small amount on the tee, patted it down, then placed a gutta-percha golf ball on top of it.

"Oh my, that is such a cute little perch you've made!" Camille said, clasping her hands together.

"Yes, you'll find the cute perch helpful," Charlie said, laughing. He took the brassie club out of the bag and handed it Camille.

"Do you know which end of the club to grip?" he asked.

"I'm just a woman and couldn't possibly figure out something so complicated," she said, putting the back of her hand to her forehead and feigning fainting.

When he tried to give her additional advice, she put her finger to her lips, shushing him. She then raised the clubhead to her lips and said, "Now you be a good boy and don't make me look silly." She took her stance, wiggled her hips for Charlie's benefit, then swung the club back and through, completely missing the ball and causing a nearby squirrel to scamper up a tree. "This game is evil!" she cried out, causing Charlie to bend over in laughter.

They had a wonderful time through the first eight holes as Charlie made two birdies, and Camille made friends with two chipmunks, a bluebird, and a deer that had wandered over. It was on the ninth tee that Camille turned to Charlie after dribbling her tee shot off the front of the tee box.

"Charlie, I have something I must tell you before we finish this lovely day on the golf course," Camille said, sitting herself down on a large boulder behind the tee box.

"Of course, Camille, have I been too overbearing with my instructions?"

"No, my instructor is brilliant, and I'm hoping that he's as understanding as he is handsome," she said, removing her bonnet and laying it on the rock next to her.

"Well, try me, Miss Hawthbaren," he said, laying the golf bag on the ground.

"Charlie, remember the man we read about in the paper this morning who's running for governor?"

"I do," he said, leaning against the far side of the boulder.

"I had a brief affair with him. Something I'm terribly ashamed of. I broke it off with him before we left on this getaway, and I must say he didn't take it well." Again raising the clubhead to her lips, she continued, "Oh, and Mr. Golf Club, did I fail to mention that he's also married?" Charlie remained silent, pondering the revelation.

"Well, Mr. Swafford?" she asked, narrowing her green eyes, and tilting her head.

"Miss Hawthbaren, I believe I saw a tall bridge spanning an alligator infested river on our way over here!" Camille picked up a pinecone and threw it at Charlie.

CHAPTER FOURTEEN
COULD IT BE HIM?
Denver, Colorado, October 11, 1900

Denver Police Chief Padraig Sullivan, a large Irishman, took great pride in being a relative of John L. Sullivan, the heavyweight boxing champion from Boston, as evidenced by a large photo of the champ hanging on the wall behind his desk. He was engrossed with examining the notes from the Mattie Silks murder. The astonishing thing to Sullivan was the ability of the perpetrator to commit such a heinous crime and disappear into the night undetected. The evidence found at the scene consisted of a small pencil with the initials CGC on it, a handwritten note, and a fake moustache in the trash can.

Into Sullivan's office walked his trusted detective, Tad Westmont, carrying an old, faded stack of newspapers, which he plopped down on Sullivan's desk.

"Excellent!" Sullivan said, removing his smoking pipe and leaning forward in his chair.

"Yes, sir! The Denver Public Library has quite a collection of newspapers. This London paper is dated November 10, 1888. According to the medical examiner, the murders of the Canonical Five were perpetrated by a left-handed individual. The sick bastard certainly did a number on Mary Jane Kelly," Westmont said, lowering his tall, thin frame down in a chair facing Sullivan.

"Does the Mattie Silks murder have both the left-handed angle of attack and the incision patterns on the eyelids of the victims in common?" asked Sullivan.

Westmont confirmed they did indeed.

"What's the best guess on the pencil that was found?"

Westmont's best guess was that the pencil came from a golf course and that given the fact that there were not yet many courses in metropolitan areas, it most likely would be from the Chicago Golf Club. "Well, that certainly gives us something to go on. After our meeting go over to Union Station. I want the name of every passenger that has arrived from Chicago in the last week."

"On it, Chief. Do you plan on making the note found at the Mattie Silk murder public?" Westmont asked.

"I've got a meeting with the district attorney and mayor in fifteen minutes. What I don't want is hysteria and panic among the citizens of Denver if we suddenly announce that Jack the Ripper has taken up residence right under our noses."

"Chief Sullivan, just imagine how good it would look if we were able to capture Jack the Ripper!"

"Indeed, Westmont; if we are able to apprehend the world's most wanted killer, the citizens of Denver will cover our capitol dome in gold!"

CHAPTER FIFTEEN
BLESS THE BEAST
Chicago, Illinois, October 9, 1900

Scotland Yard inspector and US Open Golf Champion Harry Vardon's eyes scanned the street outside the Chicago office of the American Tobacco Company. He took note of two gentlemen leaning against a newly constructed streetlamp and nodded in their direction. They returned the gesture, prompting Vardon to enter the building marked American Tobacco Company, Est. 1874.

Vardon stepped off the elevator on the sixteenth floor and was met by Buchanan Duke's secretary, Miss Hall. She ushered Vardon into a cavernous office furnished with just the type of niceties one might expect from a man worth millions of dollars.

"Hello, Mr. Vardon!" Duke said, rising from behind a sprawling cherrywood desk that was uncluttered and featured photographs of his brother Benjamin, who was vice president of the company, and his father, Washington Duke, who started the company back in 1874. Dressed in a black suit with gold cuffs, Duke had the look of a man who could make one's life either wonderful or miserable, depending on which column of his personal ledger you fell on.

"Before we get started, Mr. Vardon, let me congratulate you on your US Open victory at my very own Chicago Golf Club. I regret that I was not able to attend the tournament as I was unexpectedly called to New York on business."

Vardon thanked Buchanan for his kind words and complimented his fair city for having patrons at the event who exhibited an astute knowledge of the game. He also pointed out that he was bound for Denver, in a matter of hours.

"Ah yes, Denver. What a splendid city! Do you happen to know Lord Dunraven from England?"

"Yes, I made his acquaintance in Muirfield, Scotland, after winning my first Open Championship four years ago," Vardon answered. Duke explained that in 1883, Dunraven invited him and his wife to stay at his Estes Park Hotel. During their stay Dunraven insisted that they join him on a big-game hunting trip in the surrounding mountains. Duke boasted of bagging a mountain lion and several bears there and motioned to the wall on the far side of the office, where the heads of a mountain lion, black bear, and buffalo were suspended, their eyes glued to the proceedings.

"Harry, getting down to the business at hand, I'd like you to endorse our cigarettes here in America. I'm fully aware that you are currently under contract with the Ogden Cigarette Company in the UK; however, I don't see a conflict of interest since we don't currently market our products in England." Vardon squirmed ever so slightly in his chair.

"I must admit that I have not read the details of my current contract," Vardon responded. "May I ask, has your company conducted any studies on the health effects of tobacco?" Vardon asked while returning the stares from the eyeballs on the wall.

"Harry, I can assure you there are no health risks associated with smoking. In fact, it has been suggested that tobacco consumption adds physical vitality. Afterall, if smoking were bad for one's health, it would also be bad for business," Duke said, pushing the cigar box in Vardon's direction.

"Perhaps you're right!" Vardon said, taking a cigar and sliding it into his breast pocket. "However, I regret to inform you, Buchanan, that I'm not here to accept a business deal, but to assist your native law enforcement officials in bringing you to justice."

"What on earth are you talking about, Mr. Vardon?" At that moment the two federal officials who were earlier positioned on the street burst into the room with Miss Hall chasing and waving her arms.

"Mr. Duke, you are under arrest for illegal big-game poaching on federal land," a tall federal agent shouted while holding up his Federal Department of Wildlife badge.

"Gentlemen," Vardon said, standing up with conviction. "I have a train to catch, so I'll leave Mr. Duke in your care. As you can plainly see, the unblinking evidence in this case hangs on the wall for everyone here to see."

CHAPTER SIXTEEN
A PROBLEM

Denver, Colorado, October 11, 1900

Henry Wolcott sat in his downtown office of the Boston and Colorado Smelting Works and pondered what he should do about Miss Camille Hawthbaren. He brooded over the fact that not only would he not be warmed by her soft lips, but she could derail his aspirations to gain the governor's office. The delicate part of the equation was that he needed the support and influence of her father to win the governor's race.

"Mr. Wolcott, Mr. Woodward is here to see you."

"Ah yes, send him in, Beth."

The two men exchanged handshakes. After some preliminary chatter about Woodward's law practice and his most recent round of golf at Overland Country Club, which included a hole-in-one on the par three second hole, the two got down to business. "Is everything set for the exhibition match tomorrow with Vardon?" Wolcott asked.

"Indeed, Walter Fairbanks will be returning tonight from a funeral he was unexpectedly called away to attend."

"Excellent! And what about that ox, J. R. Cuddling?" Wolcott inquired. "Have you had contact with him after that impressive display of strength at the Denver Club?"

Woodward replied that an associate of his had spotted Cuddling at the High Peeks Saloon the night of Mattie Silks's murder. He was involved in what appeared to be a high-stakes card game.

"Have they taken anyone into custody for the Silks's murder?" Wolcott asked while putting a match to the tip of his cigar and pouring a measure of brandy into two crystal shot glasses.

"Let me remind you, Henry, that any information exchanged between us must be held in the strictest confidence and not travel beyond the walls of this office." Woodward went on to explain that investigators found a note at the scene that incredibly, was signed "Jack the Ripper," and the only hard evidence found was a small pencil with CGC inscribed on it and a fake moustache. "Chief Sullivan is conducting some comparisons with the notes that were mailed to Whitechapel Police and the London newspapers twelve years ago to determine its authenticity." *Jack the Ripper—perhaps he is the answer to all my prayers: getting rid of Miss Hawthbaren, winning the governorship, and becoming the most famous citizen in Denver, by delivering Jack the Ripper to local law enforcement,* Wolcott thought, raising his brandy glass to his smiling lips.

CHAPTER SEVENTEEN
THE EXHIBITION

Denver, Colorado, Overland Country Club,
October 12, 1900

Harry Vardon stood on the first tee of the Overland Golf Club. He was dressed in sporty attire that included a checkered cap, black trousers, a white shirt, and a tan vest. His caddie J. R. Cuddling wore a simple pair of gray pants and an extra-large, long-sleeved white shirt stretched tight by his jumbo frame. The assembled gallery, made up of members of the club and local businessmen, alternated their gazes between Vardon and Cuddling, unable to decide who was the more impressive figure.

Vardon was extremely glad to have Cuddling back in the fold. The gallery included Nathanial Hawthbaren, his wife, and the handsome couple, Camille Hawthbaren and Charlie Swafford, who were locked arm in arm. Henry Wolcott was the acting referee for the match. Vardon won the coin flip and teed off first, hitting a lovely drive, high into the air, with a stylish swing, which drew ohs and aahs from the gallery.

As the ball rolled down the fairway, Camille turned to Charlie and said. "Just like I would do it, sweetie!"

The match stood even after three holes at level par, yet on the fourth hole, Vardon's mashie niblick approach bounded over the green and into the spectators. The ball came to rest at Camille's feet. Vardon walked across the green and down the slight embankment. When he saw Camille and Charlie flanking his ball, he beamed at Camille and offered up his English manners.

"Please accept my apologies, pretty lady, for this poorly executed shot!" Vardon said, while Cuddling set the bag down next to Charlie.

"No need, Mr. Vardon; I've been known to hit a wayward shot myself," Camille responded, eliciting laughter from everyone within earshot, including Vardon.

"Mr. Vardon, we are so honored to have you in Denver, and congratulations on your US Open victory," Charlie offered, squeezing his arm around his lovely escort.

"Charlie Swafford, what on earth are you doing here?" Vardon queried while waiting for Fairbanks to play a recovery shot left-handed from underneath a cottonwood tree.

"It's been a journey indeed, Mr. Vardon, from Whitechapel to Denver."

Vardon pulled his niblick from the bag in preparation for playing the delicate pitch shot. He walked back up to the crest of the slope to gauge the shot, then returned, whistling an old Irish jig. Without delay he lofted a delicate pitch up onto the green. All eyes followed the ball as it rolled true down the slope, coming to rest a scant foot away from the hole. With the crowd applauding, Vardon turned to Charlie.

"I'd be delighted if you and your lovely escort would linger after the match for a drink." With that Vardon hurried onto the green, where he routinely rolled the ball into the hole for his par.

After the four men hit their tee shots on the twelfth hole, Vardon hurried his stride to catch up with Walter Fairbanks, who seemed to always be out ahead of the others, his head down in what one could interpret as either concealment or concentration. Vardon caught up to his fellow Englishman and walked next to him for several strides in silence before asking, in a friendly manner, what occupation he held in England before coming over to the States.

"I worked for a short time in the entertainment business and in the medical field after that," Fairbanks answered. Vardon went on to ask Fairbanks if his work ever required him to travel to the east end of London.

"Mr. Vardon, are you here to play golf or engaged in idle chatter, which does a disservice to your opponent? Now, may I ask for a modicum of sportsmanship, or would you like to continue to distract me from the task at hand?"

"No, you are entirely correct, Mr. Fairbanks; concentrate away, because there's really only going to be one outcome to our match."

"And that is, Mr. Vardon?"

"I'm going to discover the real you, Mr. Fairbanks."

"Mr. Vardon if you can do that I'd be eternally grateful," replied Fairbanks moving on ahead

CHAPTER EIGHTEEN
ADMISSION OF GUILT
Overland Country Club, October 12, 1900

When the last putt of the match tumbled to the bottom of the hole, Vardon prevailed, shooting sixty-eight to his two opponents' best ball score of seventy-one. All parties shook hands after the final flagstick was replaced, except for Vardon and Fairbanks, who awkwardly avoided each other. When Cuddling shook Wolcott's hand, a note was pressed into Cuddling's palm.

Camille and Charlie sat with her parents inside Overland's unique clubhouse, which featured a bar that spanned the entire length of the building. They were sipping on mint juleps and discussing the match and the upcoming horse races when Henry Wolcott sauntered into the room.

"Hello, Reginald, how nice it is to see you and your lovely family."

"Hello, Henry, nice to see you!" Hawthbaren responded, shaking hands.

"You know Camille and my wife?

"Yes, of course," Wolcott said, bowing.

Hawthbaren introduced Charlie, explaining that he had just resettled in Colorado from London, England, and would be joining the

Denver Tramway Company in charge of city planning. "Welcome to our fine city, Mr. Swafford," Wolcott offered, while thinking how fetching Camille looked and how jealous he was that her affections now fell into a lap that was not his own.

"Thank you, Mr. Wolcott; the beauty of your state is only trumped by the beauty of my escort," Charlie responded.

"What did you think of Vardon's performance today, Mr. Swafford? From my vantage point, it appeared that he took advantage of several lucky bounces." Wolcott asked.

Camille squeezed Charlie's hand in a way that signaled, don't take the bait.

"From my vantage it appeared Mr. Vardon didn't break a sweat." Charlie countered.

"I, for one, think Mr. Vardon possesses the most pleasing swing I've laid eyes upon," Mr. Hawthbaren interjected while swinging an imaginary club from the comfort of his chair.

"Your thoughts, Camille?" Wolcott asked, no longer able to resist addressing his former lover.

"I thought Mr. Vardon played exceptionally; however, I'm keen to know how he stands on certain social issues," Camille replied while attempting to extract a mint leaf that sank to the bottom of her drink.

Wolcott pressed on. "Speaking of important women's issues, did you hear that Nellie Bly will be at the Denver Public Library next month to give a forum on issues of interest to women? Unfortunately, it will be held the same evening as the Joe Gans versus Kid Parker fight at the Denver Athletic Club, which your father and I are planning to attend. Camille, why don't you ask Mr. Swafford here to attend, as no doubt he would fit right in with the ladies." Charlie stood and took a step toward Wolcott, but Camille lurched between the two men.

"Mr. Wolcott, out of respect for my host family here, I will overlook your provocation this time, but I may not be so amiable next time."

At that moment John Russell arrived at the bar to announce that Mr. Vardon had requested to speak with Miss Hawthbaren and Mr. Swafford on the patio. Charlie enthusiastically grabbed Camille's arm, and after apologizing to Hawthbaren's and nodding curtly in Wolcott's direction, the two followed Russell out of the room.

"I want to thank you two for coming out to the exhibition today!" Vardon said, swirling the ice around in his drink. Cuddling nodded at the couple while wiping down Vardon's golf clubs with a damp towel. Before the conversation could gain more momentum, all eyes fell on Walter Fairbanks, who was now walking down a cobblestone path, leading from the clubhouse to a waiting carriage, whereupon he entered and sped away.

"Remind me, Charlie, were you with the killer of my aunt, Mary Jane Kelly, the night before her murder?"

"I was, Mr. Vardon. In fact, Mary brought you by my flat earlier that same day."

"Ah yes, I remember your landlady told us you were out celebrating your nineteenth birthday. Tell me, did you leave me the money in the envelope, as the note found in her flat indicated?

"I did not send the money, Mr. Vardon, and the police believe that it was used as a ruse to enter her flat. I did; however, to my continuing horror, provide Jack the Ripper with her whereabouts."

"Stop, Charlie; you don't have to put yourself through this!" Camille exhorted, taking Charlie's hand in hers.

Vardon winked at Camille and told Charlie to please continue.

"The day you and Mary came by, I was out drinking with my friend Phillip Andersen. We were in the Ten Bells Pub when a man dropped his journal during a melee that broke out. I took the journal home with me, and the man who lost the journal tracked me down. If I had only read the journal, I would have found out about his murderous past. He told me he was a doctor and would help Mary, so I gave him her address, thinking he would mail her some helpful literature. Tell me, Mr. Vardon, do you and Mr. Cuddling believe that Jack the Ripper is alive and here in Denver?"

"Not only do we believe that Charlie, but I believe I just played golf with him!"

CHAPTER NINETEEN
TWO BIRDS ONE STONE

Denver, Colorado, October 12,
Later that Evening

Later that evening, after the exhibition match at Overland Country Club, Henry Wolcott stood on the bank of the South Platte River, just west of downtown Denver. A full moon cast an eerie blanket of shimmer over the slow-moving water. Wolcott was dressed in the same clothing he had worn during the exhibition except for a Derringer pistol, which was concealed under his vest. He was trembling as the call of an owl echoed off in the distance. He watched a piece of driftwood float swiftly by when he heard a familiar voice behind him.

"Please resist the urge to turn around, Mr. Wolcott."

"That sounds like an invitation to be shot in the back, Mr. Cuddling."

"That is precisely where I have my revolver pointed."

"You seem to have me at somewhat of a disadvantage."

"How did you uncover my true identity?" Cuddling demanded.

"Quite accidentally, I'll assure you." Woodward admitted.

"Explain, but be brief, as my trigger finger is getting impatient."

Wolcott went on to explain that he was frequenting the Fallen Angel Bordello the night after the murder of Mattie Silks. The lady entertaining Wolcott mentioned that on the night of the Silks's murder, she was peering out of her second-story window when she caught sight of a large man nimbly climbing out of Mattie Silks's office window. Sensing an opportunity, she quickly made her way down the stairs and out into the street to follow the man. She trailed at a safe distance, tracking the man several blocks back to the Brown Palace Hotel. Once inside the hotel, she waited for the man to retrieve his key from the front desk. With a key in hand, the man strolled in her direction. She contemplated following him into the elevator when he called back over his shoulder to the front desk. "Please have fresh towels delivered to room 613."

Having a criminal record herself, she didn't take her information to the police; however, she was more than happy to supply Wolcott with the details in exchange for a generous tip. With that information Wolcott dropped into the Brown Palace the next day and, in exchange for a twenty-dollar bill, received the information that room 613 belonged to none other than J. R. Cuddling.

"That's very resourceful of you, Mr. Wolcott. I could shoot you right now, and who would be the wiser?"

"That's true; however, being in politics has given me an appreciation of covering one's back. Are you there, Mr. Hegarty?"

"Here, sir, and I have the scoundrel in my crosshairs."

Cuddling lowered his gun.

"It would seem we are at a stalemate, Mr. Wolcott. What type of deal are you looking to strike?"

"I only want you to do what your skin is already crawling to do. I want you to kill a certain young woman, and in return, I will provide you with $1,000 in gold and ensure that you have safe passage out of Denver and on to San Francisco where a fresh supply of ladies lay in wait," Wolcott explained, while thinking, *my actual plan is to renege on the deal after he fulfills his gruesome task, and turn Cuddling over to the authorities and take all the credit for bringing Jack the Ripper to justice.*

"Who is this woman who is giving you such a bother, Mr. Wolcott?"

"Camille Hawthbaren. You were quite friendly with her after the exhibition today. I want you to kill her as soon as possible, tomorrow night, in fact. If you refuse, I'm sure the chief of police would be thrilled with the information I could supply."

"You certainly seem to have me up a creek without a paddle, Mr. Wolcott. I will agree to this arrangement, given one stipulation that I commit this murder at the house of Walter Fairbanks. As Vardon is convinced, he's Jack the Ripper this maneuver will throw the police off my scent, while I make my escape. I will meet you early in the morning at the Denver Club, as we have much to plan."

CHAPTER TWENTY
ABDUCTED
Denver, Colorado, October 13, In the Evening

Camille and Charlie had dinner at the Denver Athletic Club on the evening after the Vardon exhibition. Over dinner Charlie told Camille he fell in love with her when he watched her struggle to open a cracker packet, and Camille told Charlie she fell in love with him when he put her golf ball on that silly pile of dirt.

"Do you still plan on attending the Suffrage Conference in New York?" Charlie asked, grasping her hand gently under the table.

"Mr. Swafford, I'm currently thinking of becoming a professional golfer like Mr. Vardon, and I'll need a responsible caddie. Think of it—lots of fresh air, exercise, and best of all, I'll have your complete attention!"

"Darling, I'd gladly tote your clubs and follow you to the ends of the earth, which is precisely where we'd end up with that golf game of yours!"

Camille snatched an olive off Charlie's plate in protest, then leaned across the table and planted a kiss on his cheek. Camille informed Charlie that she would indeed be attending the conference; however, she would be returning early to start her job as the first female reporter of the Rocky Mountain News, covering important social issues of the day and—who knew—maybe someday writing a book about her experiences. Charlie thought that was a splendid idea, as he would be moving to Denver and starting his new position with the Denver Tramway Company before the month's end.

It was a lovely fall evening, so after dinner Camille and Charlie took a stroll along Glenarm Place. They were exchanging moonlit kisses when they were startled by a carriage rattling up beside them. The driver called down...

"Are you Miss Hawthbaren?"

"I am indeed," she replied, startled at the question.

"Your father has suffered a heart attack at the Denver Club and has been taken to Denver General Hospital. I've been sent to escort you to the hospital along with Dr. Molnar, who is in the carriage. I'm sorry, Miss; the carriage is full; your gentleman friend will have to wait on the next carriage, which will be along momentarily."

"You go ahead, Camille!" Charlie insisted. "I'll take the next carriage and meet you at the hospital forthright."

"Love you, Charlie. I must hurry!" She scrambled into the carriage, which then raced off, causing her to crash back onto the seat. When she gathered her senses, she noticed that there was ample room for Charlie, and sitting across from her were two men. One was her former lover, and the other was someone she would've trusted with her life not six hours ago.

"Henry, Mr. Cuddling, thank god you're here; the news about my father is most distressing. Do you have an update on his condition?" she asked, frantically searching their eyes for a response. Finally, Wolcott answered.

"Your father is in fine condition. In fact, he better be, as I'll need his energy to pave our way to the governor's mansion. I left him at the club no more than an hour ago," Wolcott said, looking out the window at the late-night revelers. *My god, this is going to be harder than I expected; however, it's too late to turn back now,* he thought to himself.

"Mr. Cuddling, what on earth is going on here?"

"Miss Swafford, I take no pleasure in what is about to transpire on this most regrettable of evenings," Cuddling said, looking down to avoid eye contact.

"So this isn't about my father, is it?" Does it have something to do with Charlie and myself?"

"Regrettably so, Miss Hawthbaren," Cuddling said.

"So you're going to hold me for ransom? That is so despicable!" Cuddling uncrossed his arms then slid open the ceiling panel and called up.

"Driver, take us to the residence of Mr. Walter Fairbanks, 900 East 17th Avenue, and make haste!"

CHAPTER TWENTY-ONE
RESCUE

Denver, Colorado, October 13, Nearing Midnight

There was no carriage following the one that took Camille away. Swafford had to scramble over to California Street to find another carriage heading in the direction of the hospital. Upon arriving at the hospital, he immediately made his way over to the reception desk and inquired about Mr. Hawthbaren's condition. He was told that there was in fact no Mr. Hawthbaren admitted, and they had not seen a woman come in fitting Camille's description. Nor did they have any record of a doctor by the name of Molnar being on staff.

Charlie now feared foul play and, using a public phone in the hospital lobby, dialed the Brown Palace Hotel and requested to be connected to Harry Vardon's room. Upon being connected he explained as calmly as possible to Vardon the events that transpired regarding Camille's abduction.

"This is very serious, Charlie; I fear that Miss Hawthbaren may be in the clutches of Jack the Ripper. Make haste and meet me in the Brown Palace lobby, and I will round up Police Chief Sullivan along with Mr. Cuddling and meet you here!" Charlie hung up the phone and ran through the hospital lobby to the cheers of encouragement from the assembled staff.

When Swafford arrived at Brown Place, he was met by Vardon and Police Chief Sullivan. The three men sat down in the hotel lobby in a state of agitation, while the hotel guests milled about, oblivious to the life-and-death nature of the unfolding events.

"If anything happens to Camille, it will kill me!" Charlie lamented, lowering his head into his trembling hands. *How could I have allowed her to get on that carriage alone?* He lamented.

"Don't blame yourself, Charlie; this man is more cunning than a starved wolf! Where in bloody hell is my man Cuddling?" Vardon asked, scanning the hotel lobby.

"Mr. Vardon, please enlighten me if you know something that we don't in this case," Chief Sullivan said, scratching his bald head in frustration.

"Mr. Sullivan, was there a note left at the scene of the Mattie Silks's murder, identifying the killer as Jack the Ripper?" Vardon asked.

"Mr. Vardon, that evidence is not meant for public consumption, and besides, why is a golfer so interested in the details of that heinous crime?"

"Mr. Cuddling and I are also special agents of Scotland Yard, assigned with the unenviable task of bringing England's own Jack the Ripper to justice." Vardon pulled a Scotland Yard Inspector's badge from his breast pocket and held it at arm's length in front of Sullivan. "I'm quite certain of the identity of Jack the Ripper, and I only need Mr. Cuddling to provide the final piece of the puzzle."

"For god's sake, Mr. Vardon, I can visually identify Jack the Ripper; we can't waste any more time," Charlie insisted, running his fingers through his thick mane of hair, and looking physically ill.

"Mr. Sullivan, let's continue without further delay to the residence of Mr. Walter Fairbanks at 900 E. 17th Avenue as quickly as possible."

"Indeed, Mr. Vardon; inspector Westmont is outside waiting in the motorcar. Mr. Swafford, I pray for your sake that Mr. Vardon's hunch is correct!" With that the three men dodged around the hotel's guests in the lobby and out of the Brown Palace.

CHAPTER TWENTY-TWO
CATCH ME IF YOU CAN

Denver, Colorado, October 13, 1900
(Stroke of Midnight)

Camille was jolted back to consciousness by the acrid scent of smelling salts being waived under her nose. When her eyes came into focus, she found herself lying on a bearskin rug in a room illuminated by a healthy fire crackling away on the other side of the room. The scene had the colors, sounds and smells of romance, yet the reality of murder. One of her wrists was handcuffed to a strong chain attached to the leg of a piano. She felt the presence of another person in the room.

"Welcome back, Miss Hawthbaren. I was hoping I wouldn't have to use the chloroform, yet it was the only way to expedite our plan, given the fact you tried several times to force your way out the carriage." Cuddling said from a chair situated before the fire.

"I demand an explanation, Mr. Cuddling."

At that moment Wolcott appeared from the hallway, leading to the front door. "Henry, have you gone mad? Unchain me so that I can get back to Charlie; the poor man must be paralyzed with worry!"

"First of all, my dear, Mr. Cuddling is no more. Meet Jack the Ripper, England's most flamboyant and successful murderer. From what he told me, your lover makes a nice cup of tea, and if that wasn't enough, the dunderhead gave him the whereabouts of his last victim, Mary Jane Kelly. You may also be wondering where you are. This lovely house belongs to Mr. Walter Fairbanks, and we plan on framing him with your murder."

"Murder!" she screamed, yanking on the chain. "If this is about money my father will meet your demands. Mr. Cuddling, you're Mr. Vardon's most trusted friend!"

"The association was most regrettable," Cuddling replied. "That's why I worked so hard to gain Harry's confidence. After all, who better catch me than myself. Don't you agree Mr. Wolcott?"

"Enough, Mr. Cuddling; if I'm not mistaken, the midnight train to San Francisco leaves in just over an hour. I see your knife on the table. Now take it and cut her throat so that you can catch your train, and I can officially begin my campaign for governor."

"This is madness!" Camille screamed, again yanking on the chain with her full might.

"Mr. Wolcott, you seem to think killing someone is an easy thing to do. Why don't you have the first crack at Miss Hawthbaren? If you slit her throat correctly, she will lose consciousness in a minute and bleed out in less than five."

"Mr. Cuddling, may I remind you of our deal? Now kill this woman, so we can both get the hell out of here!"

"I suppose it wouldn't be very sporting of an Englishman to go back on his word," Cuddling said, picking up the sharp kitchen knife from the table next to his chair. He walked over to Camille and knelt next to her. Camille didn't struggle.

"Please, Mr. Cuddling, spare my life; I'm so in love!"

"Close your eyes and count to three, Miss Hawthbaren; I'll make sure you don't suffer, as I'm very experienced at this sort of thing."

"I'll die with my eyes open!" she said defiantly, but as Cuddling steadied her head with his powerful hand, she closed her eyes and thought of Charlie.

At that moment Charlie came charging into the room from the hallway and tackled Cuddling to the floor. He was immediately followed by Vardon and Chief Sullivan. Wolcott tried to make a run for the back door; however, Vardon quickly corralled him, and Westmont applied handcuffs.

"Bloody balls Harry! It's about time you joined the party! Do I not only have to chase down your errant shots on the golf course, but your suspects as well?" Cuddling called out from underneath Swafford, who was now in procession of the knife.

"Mr. Cuddling, I should have known you were ahead of the game. Good work, old boy!" Vardon called out.

Swafford rolled off Cuddling and scrambled over to Camille, who was unhurt except for a red mark on her throat made by the dull side of the kitchen knife.

"Charlie, I think I have some good material with which to write my first newspaper article," she managed to say, wrapping her free arm around him.

"Would you please explain things, Mr. Vardon, before I have everyone here thrown in jail? Is this not Jack the Ripper here that we saw with a knife to this young woman's throat?" Sullivan questioned.

"Chief Sullivan, give Mr. Cuddling the chance to set the record straight. Mr. Cuddling, please continue," Vardon said, crossing his arms and leaning up against the wall.

"I'm not saying anything until I speak with Mr. Woodward, my lawyer," Wolcott protested as Westmont handed him off to another police officer who just arrived on the scene after subduing Wolcott's accomplice Mr. Hegarty, who was outside in preparation of ambushing Cuddling when he exited the house.

"Henry was instructing Mr. Cuddling here to slit my throat when you arrived!" Camille shouted.

Cuddling raised himself off the floor, dusted himself off, and straightened his tie before beginning.

"This manhunt that lasted twelve years and has taken Mr. Vardon and me across Europe and America can now mercifully conclude."

"Detective Snyder, take Mr. Wolcott outside while we finish up here. Please continue, Mr. Cuddling," Sullivan instructed.

Cuddling summarized his actions by explaining to the assembled the following.

After the exhibition match Wolcott passed Cuddling a note, which requested a meeting later that evening. He armed himself and met Wolcott at the appointed time and place. There, Wolcott explained to Cuddling that he had an eyewitness who placed Cuddling at Mattie Silks's murder scene.

"And how do you explain being at the scene of the murder, Mr. Cuddling?" Sullivan pressed.

Cuddling continued to explain that, given Jack the Ripper's past, he was confident that their suspect might make an appearance at the Fallen Angel Bordello house, so he began snooping around there to see if he could gather any intelligence. Sure enough, he spoke to a man who was there the day Mattie Silks's bodyguards were overpowered by an imposing figure who came in off the street. The witness explained the man in question engaged in a conversation with one of the lady entertainers who worked there. Prior to the scuffle and after removing a strange object from his soup, the witness heard the man say that he would be paying a visit to Mattie Silks later that evening.

Cuddling returned to the High Peaks Saloon that night and began playing cards and watching the front door for any sign of the man in question. When no one arrived through the front door matching the man's description, Cuddling made his way back to Silk's office and picked the lock to gain entry. Cuddling found Silks's body lying on the floor with her throat slashed and blood pooled around the body. The window was half open. He bent over

Silks's lifeless body and noticed not only the note but also the small pencil he had used to mark Vardon's scorecard at the US Open, and he remembered that he'd forgotten to retrieve the pencil off the table after signing his name on the newsletter at the Denver Club. The killer evidently planted the pencil as evidence to implicate Cuddling in the murder.

Just as he was eyeing the handwriting on the note next to the body, he heard footsteps outside the door, so he quickly crawled out through the window and made his way back to the Brown Palace Hotel and room 613 to take a hot bath and ponder his next move. Little did he know that he was being followed by an overly curious resident of the house of ill repute.

"That's a fantastic story, Mr. Cuddling!" Sullivan said looking over at Vardon, who was scratching his chin in contemplation.

"Mr. Cuddling, let's hole out the final putt on this ordeal. Where is the man who owns this house that we've been hunting for the past twelve years?" Vardon asked.

"Gentlemen, Jack the Ripper, who has been living in Denver for the past two years under the assumed name of Walter Fairbanks, is safely tied up in the basement. We had quite a tussle earlier this evening. His strength is that of the devil, and he almost had me dead to rights in a reverse English chokehold."

"Westmont, take your revolver and go down in the basement and guard the killer, as we will be down as soon as we get Miss Hawthbaren unchained."

Westmont followed Chief Sullivan's command and hurried over to the basement stairs, where he turned on the light before ambling down. Cuddling was unlocking the chain that held Camille when Westmont stormed back up the basement stairs and reappeared, huffing and puffing.

"He's gone! There's a window broken out down there with glass on the floor. This note was on the floor next to this discarded rope, which he dangled as evidence." Vardon secured the note from Westmont and read it out loud.

Gentlemen,

Congratulations on finding your old friend. You almost had me, except you forgot one important detail. Before I was Jack the Ripper, I was Slippery Sam, London's greatest escape artist. Claire Davis will join me in retirement, as my quiet heart now belongs to her.

P.S. *- If Charlie Swafford is within earshot—keep your chin up, old boy. In giving me Mary Jane Kelly's address, you saved a lucky woman from a horrible death.*

Happy Trails, JTR

CHAPTER TWENTY-THREE
SOUL TO REST

London, England, March 1937

Camille had her arm hooked under Charlie's as they sat near the back of the gathered guests at Saint Andrew's Church in Totteridge, London. Charlie patted his wife's hand.

"It's a shame Mr. Cuddling couldn't be here for Harry's funeral, yet I think it's brilliant that his son Bode will be giving Mr. Vardon's eulogy.

"Camille, do you see that man taking his seat up front?"

"Yes, I do, darling, and that reminds me that when we get back to Denver, you must get those eyes of yours checked, as one of these days you're going to come home from the golf course and hug the maid instead of me," she responded, adjusting the blanket that was warming their legs.

"Yes, sweetie, all in good time." Charlie explained that the man taking his seat was Francis Ouimet, who had defeated Vardon in a playoff for the 1913 US Open at the tender age of nineteen. A victory full of irony, as he had defeated Harry Vardon and Ted Ray in a playoff at the very same course that he grew up caddying on and lived next door to, the Country Club at Brookline.

"Do you think this Mr. Ouimet was as good of a caddie as Mr. Cuddling was?" she asked, while checking her makeup in a small pocket mirror.

"Honey, the question should be, was he a better golfer than Harry Vardon? Do you suppose he could be sailing home to New York with us on the Queen Mary?"

She was about to answer when she suddenly dropped the makeup mirror in her lap.

"Look who else just joined the party, darling," she whispered in his ear. Charlie caught sight of Henry Wolcott taking a seat on the other side of the aisle, just as the Anglican minister approached the podium to begin the service.

While all this played out in front of Charlie and Camille, a woman in her early twenties sat silently in the back row, watching the proceedings. She had reddish hair, wide-set hazel eyes, and a strong chin. Her frame was large for a woman, yet feminine around the edges. She knew not another soul attending the service, yet her association with the departed was a special one, that only two people in attendance knew of, and one of them was dead.

CHAPTER TWENTY-FOUR
CRUISING HOME
Southampton, England, June 1937,
After Vardon's Funeral

Commadore Robert B. Irving was overjoyed at being the captain of the HMS Queen Mary. He was most proud of the eleven hundred crew members, who pampered the more than two thousand passengers. Irving wanted each passenger to feel as if they had experienced a slice of life on the high seas that could not be matched by any other transatlantic liner. Taking three and a half years to build, the liner had been in service less than a year when Camille and Charlie made their way up the gangplank. After stepping onto the foredeck, the couple shook the hand of Captain Irving.

"Mr. and Mrs. Swafford, hailing from Denver, welcome aboard the Queen Mary for your return trip to the US. I hope your stay in England was an enjoyable one. Captain Irving at your service."

"Captain Irving, thank you for the kind greeting. How on earth do you know who we are?" Charlie inquired, looking at Camille in surprise. Captain Irvine explained that he had a photographic memory, which was passed down from his grandfather, who was a cartographer for the government.

"That's fascinating, Captain. May I quickly test your memory?" asked Camille.

"Sweetie, let's just keep moving, the captain is a very busy man!"

"No worries, Mr. Swafford. Please continue, Mrs. Swafford."

"Very well, my husband would like to know if there's a Mr. Francis Ouimet on your manifest?"

Indeed, a Mr. Ouimet had booked passage only yesterday in the last remaining double-occupancy, first-class cabin, #641. He is sharing that cabin with a Mr. Walter Hagen, who is returning to the US after leading the US team to a victory in the Ryder Cup in Southport, England. Camille put her hands together and bowed to the captain in admiration. *This man would be formattable at cards!* Charlie thought. "One more, Captain, and I'm a believer," Camille said as she peered back over her shoulder at the line of passengers waiting. "Henry Wolcott?"

"No, Miss Swafford, that name is not on our passenger's list."

"Move along, miss; who do you think you are, the blooming Queen of England?" shouted a rotund man, with a patchy gray beard standing in line with his frazzled wife and two hungry-looking children in tow.

As the Swafford's hurried on, Captain Irving called after them, "Please join me for dinner tonight at the captain's table!"

CHAPTER TWENTY-FIVE
ROOMMATES
North Atlantic, Out to Sea

The Queen Mary's four huge propellers, each twenty feet wide and weighing thirty-five tons, spun at two revolutions per second and were powered by four steam turbines and twenty-four boilers. Already a hundred miles out to sea, the ship would dock in New York in three days.

Bode Cuddling, fresh off giving the eulogy at Harry Vardon's funeral, sat at the small writing desk in Cabin 315. He was writing down words on the cabin's stationery. Sentiments that could express either an explanation, or a confession depending on the spirit of its delivery. He set the pen down and reflected on his father J. R. Cuddling, who died in 1927 in a plane crash on a flight from London to Dublin, Ireland. The bodies of the pilot and his father were never recovered from the clutches of the Irish Sea.

Bode's reflection was interrupted by a commotion outside his cabin door. He stood and ran his fingers through his long blond hair just as a porter pushed the door open. Standing at the threshold was Miss Catherine George of Boston. Upon seeing Bode she hesitated. A look of puzzlement came over her as she pulled the door back toward her to confirm the cabin number.

"Excuse me, sir, I believe this is my cabin." The porter holding the luggage was also concerned, but more about how the evolving situation might affect his tip.

"I'm so sorry, Miss…?"

"George!" she replied, turning to the porter, and giving him an annoyed look.

"My name is Bode Cuddling, and I've already spoken to the deck mate about this situation, Miss George, as I was fully expecting room 315 to be a single cabin as well. There was a mix-up of some sort, and they assigned us both to this double cabin. Don't just stand here, young man; put Miss George's bags down and go fetch Steward Spears," Cuddling demanded while he removed a silver dollar from his breast pocket and deposited it in the calloused palm of the porter, who put the suitcase inside the door and scurried off.

"Well, it appears we have a situation on our hands, Mr. Cuddling."

"Please call me Bode, Miss George."

"Very well then, Bode; you may call me Catherine," she said, her eyes now fully taking in the man who was sharing in the awkward moment. "Wait, are you not the man who gave the eulogy for Mr. Vardon today?"

Bode confirmed as much and was about to ask Catherine if she enjoyed the service when Steward Spears appeared in the doorway. He was thin as a rail with pale blue eyes and what appeared to be the beginnings of a red moustache riding his top lip.

"Mr. Cuddling and Miss George, believe me when I say the captain and the entire Cunard Line apologize for the room mix-up!"

"Your apology is accepted. Now if you'll just show Mr. Cuddling to another room, all will be forgiven."

"I'm afraid it's not quite so easy, Miss George. The ship is completely booked; there are no other rooms available," he replied, while flashing Cuddling a complicit glance and thinking, *I better not loose my job over this arrangement.*

"That's quite unacceptable, Mr. Spears! Certainly there must be a comfortable cot somewhere that will serve Mr. Cuddling's needs just fine, as I need to unpack and get ready for dinner."

"I'm afraid that's against ship regulations, Miss George. As you can see, the beds are separated by a partition that can be extended. If you can make do, the captain has agreed to give you both a voucher for 50 percent off your next steerage on the Cunard Line. He is also extending an invitation to join him at his table for dinner tonight."

"We accept!" Bode said while reaching for Miss George's luggage.

CHAPTER TWENTY-SIX
CAPTAIN'S TABLE
North Atlantic, Summer, 1937

"Darling, will you please wear that cologne you packed?"

"Which one?" Charlie asked as he thumbed through the ties at the bottom of his suitcase.

Camille walked up behind him, putting her arms around him, and whispered in his ear, "You know the one you wore when we met in Estes Park."

"Camille, why do you like that aftershave so much?" Charlie asked.

"I like it because it takes me back to a time and place that was so fresh, and young, and sensual."

"That's what makes you a great writer Camille, you have sentimentality," he said removing the aftershave and holding it up in the air.

"Camille, if your readers knew what a tigress you are, they would turn away from your articles blushing."

Charlie was proud of the writing career Camille had carved out in Denver. When Charlie accepted his position with her father's transportation company in 1900, Camille, true to form, wasted little time in forging her own identity as a writer and activist. Her first big story was quite naturally the article she penned about Jack the Ripper and his narrow escape from justice. She did a masterful job of interviewing both Harry Vardon and J. R. Cuddling regarding their attempts to apprehend the villain over the intervening years, including one where they had him corned in a monastery in France, only to have him escape under their noses dressed as a nun. However, the biggest response to Camille's three-installment piece, which was published in the *Rocky Mountain News* in 1901, came from readers, who were fascinated by Charlie's encounter with London's most famous murderer. They wanted to know what Jack the Ripper was like. What did he look like? Was he really that cunning? Some women wanted to know where they could send love letters addressed to JTR.

Another of Camille's contributions to moving the country forward was her steadfast support for the Nineteenth Amendment to the US Constitution, which guaranteed women the right to vote on a national level in 1920. In 1918, fellow Denverite Molly Brown, a.k.a. "The Unsinkable Molly Brown," who had survived the sinking of the RMS Titanic in 1912, traveled to Washington, DC, to meet with then-President Woodrow Wilson.

Camille had a private meeting with Wilson in the Oval Office and rightly judged that Wilson was a man averse to confrontation and coercion. She took a different tack and didn't mention women's suffrage at the outset of their meeting. As the conversation between the two progressed, Wilson became impressed with Camille's knowledge of politics and world affairs.

"Mrs. Swafford, if those women out there picketing in front of the White House knew as much about geopolitics as you, I'd be more inclined to agree with their position."

Camille found her opening and posed a direct yes-or-no question to the president.

"Mr. President, could you see in the future how an informed women's electorate could be a powerful ally to anyone seeking the presidency?"

Wilson smiled, removed his glasses, leaned forward, and replied, "I do, indeed, Mrs. Swafford—I do, indeed!"

It was six o'clock sharp that evening when Charlie and Camille lowered themselves into two of the ten chairs situated around the captain's table. When everyone was at last in their respective chairs, the captain stood and proceeded to introduce the guests one by one, moving to his left for each new introduction. There was Mr. Bond, President of the Royal Bank of Scotland; Mr. Tappers, the overseer of the Royal Mint; Mr. Aaron Gardner, St. Andrew's University President; and Margaret Lockwood, English actress extraordinaire, who was on her way to Hollywood to star in a Paramount Pictures film *Rulers of the Sea* with Douglas Fairbanks, Jr. When he came to the seats of Bode Cuddling and Catherine George, he took a deep breath.

"Ladies and gentlemen. Here, before me, sit the winners of Queen Mary's most congenial award. They both made a personal sacrifice in the interest of the smooth operations of the Queen Mary. Mr. Bode Cuddling of London and Miss Catherine George of Boston."

Bode smiled and nodded in the captain's direction, while Catherine buried her eyes in the napkin on her lap.

"Finally, on my right we have Mr. Francis Ouimet, who's returning to the States after attending legendary English golfer Harry Vardon's funeral, and Mr. Walter Hagen, a professional golfer, whose American Ryder Cup team recently defeated our boys at the Southport and Ainsdale Golf Club to win back the Ryder Cup."

After dinner and before dessert, the captain was asked for his secret to his amazing memory.

"A photographic memory is a rare thing; indeed, however, here's a tip that can help anyone remember almost anything. It's called association. Take Charlie and his lovely wife, Camille, here. Now for Camille imagine she is riding atop a camel—think Camille—and then picture the poor beast suffering a charley horse—think Charlie. Set that image in your mind, and you can't forget Camille and Charlie."

Not wanting to waste the moment and quite frankly totally out of character, Charlie stood from his chair and announced, "And if you want to remember our last name, picture me swatting my wife over the head with a flyswatter—think Swafford," whereupon he took his napkin and flogged her over the head a couple of times for visual reinforcement. When no one laughed and the captain frowned, like a teacher confronting an unruly student, Charlie melted back into his chair.

After dinner Captain Irving asked Charlie and Camille if they would like to see the latest innovation of the Cunard Line. He escorted them to the top deck of the ship and walked them back to the stern. There, in an area specially constructed with black walnut decking and a wooden pegboard to hang hats and towels on, was what appeared to be a small swimming pool with steam rising from it.

"What on earth, Captain?" Charlie said, wrapping his arm around his wife's waist for fear she might fall into the steamy caldron."

"Is this where the staff does the dishes?" Camille questioned.

Irving assured the couple that there were no pots and pans at the bottom and that, in fact, it was a special blend of mineral water and body salts heated to a temperature of 105 degrees.

"It's not officially open until our return voyage; however, if you're so inclined, I'd like for the both of you to try it and give me your opinion of its restorative powers," said the captain. He went on to elaborate that one should refrain from drinking alcohol while immersed and not exceed ten minutes of exposure, as he would like to avoid any reputation of cooking his passengers. "Now, I will bid you a good evening, as I have to check in with my first officer on the bridge and make sure we don't veer off course and miss America."

CHAPTER TWENTY-SEVEN
THE HAIG
North Atlantic, Almost Home

After dinner at the Captain's table, Walter Hagen and Francis Ouimet were enjoying a brandy in the ship's tavern.

"Walter, congrats on regaining the Ryder Cup from Great Britan! It would appear your friend Sarazen, the 'Old Squire,' still has some juice left in the tank!"

"Thank you, Francis! The boys arrived with a fire already tanning their backsides from losing four years ago. I just tried to keep them loose by encouraging them to visit the local pubs and make some life-long friends. As you know, I always played my best golf when nursing a hangover."

Hagen and Ouimet were the original "odd couple." Hagen was bold, brilliant, and brash. Ouimet was measured, consistent, and controlled. Their different approaches to championship golf could be summed up by how each handled themselves on the eve of the final round of a major championship.

On the evening of the final round of the 1913 US Open, Ouimet spent the night at home in quiet reflection and was in bed by 10:00 p.m. In contrast on the night before the final round of the 1926 PGA Championship against Leo Diegel, Hagen was spotted by a sports reporter late into the night at a local pub with a drink in one hand and an attractive blonde in the other. The writer recognized Hagen and scolded him by pointing out that, while Hagen was out living it up on the town, his opponent was safe in his hotel room, enjoying a good night's sleep. Hagen smiled at the reporter, and after giving the blonde a peck on the cheek, responded, "Diegel may be home and in bed, but I can guarantee you he isn't sleeping."

When the drinks finally arrived, Ouimet excused himself, saying he was tired and was going to go back to the cabin and read some scripture before retiring. Hagen bade his friend good night, and as Hagen was watching him exit out of the tavern, he caught sight of Margaret Lockwood, leaning up against the ship's guardrail, smoking a cigarette. She was occupied gazing out onto the vast Atlantic, which was now illuminated by a full moon. *The evening just got a whole lot more interesting,* Hagen thought to himself, as he plucked the spare drink off the bar and made his way out to the woman in waiting.

"Walter Hagen at your service," he said calmly, while setting the two drinks on the railing and extracting a cigarette of his own.

She turned, fixing Hagen with her speckled brown eyes, catching the moonlight, and inhaled on her cigarette, letting the smoke slowly drift back out of her nose.

"I don't sleep with men I don't know," she replied just as casually, turning her head back out to sea.

Hagen remained silent, also taking in the sea vista.

"I said I don't sleep around; now scram!" she said more forcefully, facing him. The situation was akin to Hagen finding his ball stymied behind a tree on the final hole of a championship with no recovery in sight, so he took his medicine and put the ball back into play.

"Of course, Miss Lockwood; I too enjoy times like this to reflect alone," he said, taking the extra drink with him and moving down the railing twenty feet or so, where he put the drinks on a nearby table and continued to smoke his cigarette and enjoy the view. After a few minutes, Lockwood wandered down next to Hagen.

"Forgive my rudeness, Mr. Hagen, and congratulations on your Ryder Cup victory, although I was of course rooting for the Brits."

"Thank you, Miss Lockwood, and no apologies needed. I should have asked if you indeed wanted company. I stopped by to ask you about your latest picture, *Jury of Evidence*. I'm somewhat of a movie buff," Hagen said.

"Of course, Mr. Hagen; what did you think of it?"

"Do you want to know what I really think Miss Lockwood?"

"Yes of course!"

"I felt your character Betty Stanton was not fully developed. Your acting fell below my expectations. In my humble opinion," he added while moving away from the railing to retrieve his drink off the table.

"Well, Mr. Hagen, you certainly are not afraid to express an opinion now, are you? That said, I agree with you the character wasn't developed to the point I wanted. I implored Mr. Ince, the director, to have the character of Betty exert herself more in several scenes, and do you want to know what that twerp of a director told me?"

"Do tell!" Hagen encouraged, leaning into the conversation like an excited schoolboy.

"His response was that the leading man, Hartly Power, didn't want his role to be watered down by another strong character." Having said that, she reached into Hagen's breast pocket and removed his gold-plated cigarette holder. She removed a cigarette and raised it to her lips. "Do you mind?" she asked, sliding the cigarette holder back into place.

Hagen followed her lead by striking a match and extending it to her cigarette.

"Have you seen all of my movies, Mr. Hagen?"

"No, but I'm very interested in learning more about them; however, I'm sure you are consumed with fans wanting to talk about your movies."

"Let's talk about something else then, Mr. Hagen."

"Tell me, Miss Lockwood, if you were stuck out in the middle of that great, big ocean in a small raft all by yourself, what would you be thinking?"

"I'd be thinking that I'm belly-balls screwed, Mr. Hagen, and what would you think?"

"I'd be thinking how nice it would be to have someone like you, Miss Lockwood, to talk to."

"Ooh, I like that, Mr. Hagen. I just might have to break my rule about sleeping with strangers," she said, taking a drag on the cigarette and lifting the spare drink off the table.

"I'll be in cabin 199 if you'd like to stop by later, Mr. Hagen, and help me with a love scene that I need to do with Errol Flynn in our upcoming movie," she propositioned.

"Miss Lockwood, I don't do love scenes with strangers," Hagen replied in all seriousness. With an impish grin on her face, she leaned forward and with her free hand straightened Hagen's tie. She then turned and walked away, disappearing into the shadows.

I love women, Hagen thought to himself winking up at the moon above.

CHAPTER TWENTY-EIGHT
UNWANTED NEWS
Somewhere on the Blue Atlantic

After the tour of the hot tub, Camille and Charlie returned to their room, and just as Charlie was inserting the cabin key, they heard a voice call out from down the hallway.

"Mr. and Mrs. Swafford, one moment, please; may I have a word with you?" Bode was soon standing at their side.

"Please come inside." Charlie said as he inserted the key and pushed open their cabin door.

"Sit down Bode and let us know what's on your mind." Charlie said, pulling up a chair, while Camille sat down on the end of the bed. Cuddling lowered himself down in the chair and proceeded to remove a letter from the breast pocket of his dinner jacket.

"This is the last correspondence my father received from Mr. Vardon before his untimely death." Bode handed the letter to Charlie, before he continued on to explain its contents this way:

Vardon discovered that Walter Fairbanks, aka Jack the Ripper, and his partner, Claire Davis, were now married and living in Boston, Massachusetts, under the assumed names of Mr. and Mrs. Alfred George, MD.

"Wait, George! Is that not the name of the woman you are currently sharing a cabin with?" Camille questioned.

"Precisely, Mrs. Swafford," Cuddling said, as Charlie unfolded the letter and began reading.

"Bode, is this not great news? Now you can finally bring Jack the Ripper to justice after all these years!" Camille said, squeezing her husband's hand.

"I wish it were that easy, given that a totally unexpected variable has been inserted into the equation…I'm falling in love with the daughter of Jack the Ripper."

CHAPTER TWENTY-NINE
SOMETHING UP HIS SLEEVE
Steaming Toward the New World

It was nearing eleven o'clock in the evening when Bode Cuddling finally left Swafford's cabin and made his way back to his own.

"Do you think I convinced Bode that it's the right thing to do?" Charlie asked, slipping off his shoes and rubbing the bottoms of his feet. After a moment of silence Charlie added, "Do those five women Jack the Ripper killed not deserve justice?"

"Yes, darling, but those women are all dead now, and Catherine has her whole life ahead of her. Is this not a rather heavy cross to lay across her shoulders at such an early age?"

"As always, you make a good counterpoint," Charlie said.

"I can't possibly sleep after such an exchange; Charlie, how about you?"

"I agree. Do you want to play pinochle?" he asked.

"Darling, I've got an idea. Why don't we go up on deck and try out that hot tub thingy the captain showed us?"

"Honey, have you ever seen a lobster dropped into a pot of boiling water? No thank you."

"I trust the captain when he says we will not be boiled to death. Come on it will be fun." Charlie relented and they wrapped themselves into their robes with the Cunard Line insignia and made their way topside.

"Honey, you go first," Camille requested as the two of them stood at the edge of the tub.

"Me? This was your idea, sweetheart, so I think it only fitting that you take the maiden plunge."

"I suppose it would've been prudent to pack bathing suits," Camille said as she glanced in both directions. Camille sat down on the edge of the spa and, shedding her robe, slipped into the steamy liquid.

"Charlie, you savage beast, get in here—it's marvelous!" she said, flicking drops of hot water in his direction.

Charlie followed her lead and, removing his robe quickly, submerged.

"Darling, is this not the most romantic of scenes?" Camille asked as she looked out across the railing, taking in the enormous, black Atlantic looming behind the rising veil of steam.

"What a scene of soggy lovebirds we have here!" said Henry Wolcott, emerging from the shadows.

"Henry! What are you doing here? I checked, and you're not listed on the manifest of passengers!"

"I'm living the life of a stowaway, my dear. I have my reasons for not wanting a record of traveling on this lovely ship. It's really not too bad, as a nice Hungarian family traveling in third class has taken me under their wing. As to what I'm doing here, I'm attempting to do what no one else has been able to do, and that's find Jack the Ripper and bring him to justice dead, or alive, as they used to say back in the Old West."

"I'm looking for a small bit of information. If you give it to me, I'll let you two get back to whatever it is you're doing in there. Is there a passenger on this ship who is related to Walter Fairbanks?"

"Take your leave, Mr. Wolcott, before I climb out of here and throw you overboard, like a bag of rubbish." Charlie demanded.

"Very well then." Wolcott replied as he walked over to the two robes on the deck and, picking them up, strolled over to the ship's rail and extended the garments over the surging Atlantic eighty feet below.

"Just give me a name, and I'll return your robes."

"We'll dance naked to entertain the departing passengers before giving you any information!" Camille hollered.

CHAPTER THIRTY
BREAKING NEWS
Choppy Seas Ahead

As Camille and Charlie were sneaking back down the stairs leading to their cabin wrapped in a shower curtain, Bode and Catherine were in the ship's tavern, playing a game of cards and having coffee and apple strudel.

"Bode, I'd like to thank you for being a perfect gentleman these last thirty-six hours. If you'd be so inclined, I'd like to invite you to Boston to have dinner with my parents."

Bode, choked on his coffee.

"My goodness, I don't remember having this sort of effect on a gentleman before!" she said.

"Believe me, Catherine, your overture is most welcome, and I'd be honored to accompany you; however, there is something that I have to tell you!"

"Ah, I see. You've already been spoken for. I should've inquired as to such," she said, taking a sip of her own coffee.

Bode assured her that was not the case and adjusted his position in his chair, like a parishioner before confession and continued.

"You see, Catherine, unbeknownst to you, our two families share a unique history."

"What do you mean history?"

"Let me take a step back," Bode said. "Look out at that beautiful ocean, Catherine, and tell me what you see."

"I see someone who is very nervous about accepting a simple dinner invitation," she said, while waving the maître d' over to fill their coffee cups.

"What I'm trying to say, Catherine, is that when we look out on the fabulous Atlantic, we only see the surface, and we think it's beautiful, yet there is so much we don't see lurking beneath."

"Waiter, cancel the coffee and bring us two gin and tonics!" Catherine instructed when the waiter arrived at their table.

"Catherine, how much do you know about your father?"

"I know that he's been a good father; he was a respected surgeon before retiring ten years ago. He volunteers, loves my mother, and likes to play golf three times a week. Oh, and he enjoys chocolate chip cookies. Is that enough information for you, Mr. Cuddling?"

"There you go, Catherine; that's what I mean. That's the surface of your father's ocean."

"Oh, my word," Catherine sighed as the drinks arrived at the table.

"By the way," Bode continued. "There's an older gentleman sitting on the other side of the room who arrived shortly after we got here. He's been keeping an eye on us. Would you mind excusing yourself and, on your way to the ladies' room, give him the once over and let me know if you've ever seen him before?"

Catherine lifted her drink and, after taking a swallow, fixed Bode with her hazel eyes over the rim of her glass.

"I'll do as you order, Inspector Cuddling; however, upon my return, you will tell me what this strange fixation is that you have with my father."

Bode watched as she made her way toward the ladies' room, her hips swayed in a way that signaled her frustration with Bode. He was taken aback when she stopped at the man's table and exchanged a few words before continuing on to the restroom. When she returned to the table, Bode stood up.

"What on earth was that all about?"

"I will tell you what he said only after you explain what's going on."

"Very well then, I will come right out with it, but before I do, will you promise not to make a scene?"

"Oh, my goodness, I'm a full-grown woman; how bad could this possibly be?"

Bode plunged headfirst into the history of his father and his association with the famous golfer Harry Vardon. He began to explain the history of Jack the Ripper, but Catherine stopped him by explaining she knew all about Jack the Ripper, because her father was working on a book about the famous murderer, and that she attended Vardon's funeral on the behest of her father, who said they were old friends.

"Your father is writing a book on Jack the Ripper?" Bode asked, gulping down his entire gin and tonic.

"Yes, my father lived in London during that time and has always been fascinated by the crimes and how the killer evaded the authorities and vanished into thin air."

"Catherine, I hate to tell you this, but there is a reason why your father is so fascinated by Jack the Ripper."

"I just told you he's interested in the crimes of Jack the Ripper, because he was in London during those heinous murders. Why else would he be interested, and by the way if you do come with us for dinner, please don't chug down your gin and tonics like that; my parents will think you're a lush."

Bode reached across the table and took Catherine's hand in his.

"The reason your father is so interested in Jack the Ripper is quite simple. You're father is Jack the Ripper and he committed those murders."

Catherine snatched her hand away and stared at Bode as if he had just grown a second head. As if this wasn't shocking enough, Bode continued on.

"Your mother's real name is Claire Davis, not Polly McFarland. Your father rescued her from a brothel in Denver after putting a bodyguard in the hospital and murdering her madam."

"You, Mr. Cuddling, must be completely out of your mind! I will be in my room and am not to be disturbed." She rose from the table, picked up her drink, and emptied it over Bode's head. She stormed toward the exit and, halfway there, turned and called back to Bodie.

"By the way, my parents, Dr. and Mrs. George of Boston, never lived in Denver. And for your information, this fine gentleman sitting over here propositioned me earlier. Maybe we'll have more to talk about than my father being Jack the Ripper!" she exhorted before exiting the cocktail lounge in front of the wide eyes and burning ears of Henry Wolcott.

CHAPTER THIRTY-ONE
DEATH OF AN OLD FRIEND
One Day Out of New York

Charlie and Camille were awakened in the middle of the night by a rapping on their cabin door. Charlie shook Camille and asked if she'd hung out the Do Not Disturb sign as he requested.

"Yes, I did, darling. They can't be cleaning at this hour," she said.

Charlie rolled out of the bed and, stretching his back, made his way over to the door.

"Who is it, please?"

"It's me, Bode. Please open the door!"

"We've had a bloody, dreadful go of it this evening, Bode. Could you come back in the morning?"

"This can't wait—as I believe I just killed a man in our cabin!"

"Good god, please explain yourself!" Camille now had a blanket wrapped around her sitting on the edge of the bed, wide-eyed.

"I'll explain all of this later, but for now, please help me with the body." Charlie told Camille to stay in the room until he got back.

He quickly dressed and followed Bode back to his cabin. Bode inserted the key, and they gained entry. Once inside they found Catherine sitting on the floor, her back up against the wall. Her eyes were shut, and her chin rested on her knees. She welcomed them by extending her arm and pointing a finger at the partition, which separated the room.

"I moved the body from this side of the room to behind the screen," Catherine informed in a weary voice. Bode rolled back the screen, and Charlie stepped forward.

"Bloody Jesus, it's Mr. Wolcott!"

"You know this man, Mr. Cuddling?"

"I do. He's been a thorn in our side ever since he attempted to team up with Jack the Ripper to kill my wife!"

Catherine let out a scream.

"Has everyone on this ship gone nuttier than my mother's fruitcake?" Catherine shouted to no one in particular.

"Can someone please explain how Mr. Wolcott came to be prone on your cabin floor?" Charlie asked.

"Mr. Cuddling and I were playing cards, and, on my way to the ladies' room, he stopped me and asked if I had attended Mr. Vardon's funeral. I told him that indeed I did and that my father and Mr. Vardon were acquaintances more than thirty years ago. Then after Mr. Cuddling so eloquently informed me that my father is not in fact a respected surgeon and pillar of the community but rather a diabolical killer, this man showed up at my door and wanted to know more about my father. I told him to leave, and he became angry and forced his way into our cabin. Mr. Cuddling arrived back just as I began to struggle with the man, as I believed he was attempting to have his way with me."

"I put a shoulder into him, knocking him back against the wall," Bode explained. "He struck his head and slumped to the floor. We need to do something with the body, Mr. Swafford, as the cleaning crew will want access to the room in a few hours."

"Couldn't we just throw him overboard?" Catherine suggested.

"That's not a bad idea, Catherine!" agreed Bode.

"Miss George, to you!" she corrected.

Charlie pondered that idea before expressing his concern that if anyone caught them in the act, they could all be charged with murder. *If only we could make it look like an accident,* Charlie thought to himself.

"Wait, I've got an idea!" Charlie said. "Bode, do you have a pair of swimming trunks by chance?"

Bode answered that he did.

"I see what you're thinking, Mr. Swafford; we make it look like a drowning," Catherine said.

Charlie told them of the secluded hot tub that had not yet been opened to the public. The plan was simple, and all they needed was a swimsuit, a strong back, and a sliver of luck.

It was almost six in the morning when Charlie finally arrived back in the room to find a sleeping Camille. He shook her awake.

"I'm sorry, darling; I dozed off. What on earth happened?" she asked, straightening up in bed. Charlie explained how he had returned with Bode only to find Mr. Wolcott dead on the floor and how they executed the plan to make it look like an accident in the hot tub. She leaned her head on Charlie's shoulder. "I should never have gotten involved with him. I feel somewhat responsible for this entire fiasco."

"It was an unfortunate accident, but I can't say he didn't have it coming to him." Charlie admitted.

"Perhaps we should sneak up to the hot tub area and take a peek?" Camille suggested. Charlie agreed it might be a good idea to check on the situation and after Camille dressed, they made their way up to the level of the hot tub. On the landing they paused, leaning up against the outside door.

"Shush, I'll crack the door and take a peek," Charlie said, but before he did, the inside stairwell door behind them swung open, and onto the landing area emerged Captain Irving.

"Captain! How nice to see you!" Camille blurted, trying to muffle the panic in her voice.

"We've decided to take you up on your offer to try the hot tub!" Charlie quickly added.

"But you have your clothes on, Mr. and Mrs. Swafford," Irving said, perplexed.

"Yes, Captain, both Charlie and I are quite modest, so naturally we have our swimsuits on underneath our clothes."

"Do as you please. I was just going to check on the condition of the tub myself. I want to make sure no debris has made it into the water, as that can cause the pump that circulates the water to clog and fail. Shall we?" He gestured toward the door.

Charlie winced as he pushed the door open. What they stumbled upon was nothing any of them were prepared for. Walter Hagen and Miss Lockwood were in the middle of the tub, locked in a kiss.

The sound of the door shutting behind them broke the spell, and Miss Lockwood pulled away from her transatlantic lover and scuttled over to the side of the tub, while Hagen called over the rising steam.

"Nothing to see here, Captain. Miss Lockwood and I were simply practicing a scene in an upcoming movie. It's going to be called *The Reluctant Mermaid*."

Charlie and Camille were dumbfounded, as they truly expected to find Mr. Wolcott's body bobbing up and down in the tub like a cork.

"Ah, Mr. Hagen. Good to see you!" said the captain. "How are you and Miss Lockwood enjoying the new toy of the Cunard Line?"

"It's lovely, Captain," Miss Lockwood answered from across the tub. "Walter was just saying that he should look into the possibility of a smaller version of this steamy tub to be installed in backyards all across America."

Camille whispered in Charlie's ear, "Darling, did you check to make sure Mr. Wolcott was indeed dead?"

Much to their relief, the Captain excused himself, saying he had duties on the bridge.

"Mr. Hagen, it's truly a pleasure to see you again," Charlie said, taking Camille's hand in his.

"Miss Lockwood, I'm a fan of your movies," Camille added, waving across the tub to the actress.

"Feel free to remove your clothes and join us!" Hagen invited enthusiastically, looking at Miss Lockwood, who in turn looked at Camille and gestured her in with a wave of her hand.

"We'd like to very much." Camille said. "However, we are late for a breakfast rendezvous with Mr. Cuddling and Miss George."

Charlie finally asked Hagen if they'd encountered anyone else in or around the tub.

"Why yes, we did, Mr. Swafford. When Margaret and I arrived, there was a man sitting on the edge of the tub. He looked to be recovering his senses, as if he'd just awoken from a nap. We said hello; however, he didn't answer but instead unsteadily rose and made his way back down the stairwell."

With that information, Charlie and Camille met Bode and Catherine in the main dining room for breakfast, their last meal, before the disembarking time of noon. Camille sensed the tension between Bode and Catherine.

"Bode, I have some good and rather perplexing news to share about Mr. Wolcott."

"I take it the crew has discovered the body and are now asking questions?" Bode replied.

Charlie went on to explain the scene at the hot tub and pronounced that Wolcott was alive and kicking and was probably wondering, at this very moment, how in the hell he wound up in the ship's hot tub.

"Miss George, I do understand how the news that Bode delivered to you about your father would be both unbelievable and repulsive. There are two things we need to consider. First, my husband spent some amount of time in close proximity to Jack the Ripper and is confident that he could make a visual identification, even after all these years. Second, Jack the Ripper lived under the alias of Walter Fairbanks while in Denver. He also played in a golf exhibition with Mr. Vardon in 1900 at Overland Country Club in Denver."

"Catherine, Walter Fairbanks, aka Jack the Ripper, has two peculiarities: he plays golf left-handed and keeps a precise journal of his activities." Charlie added.

"My father plays golf right handed; he's been trying to teach me for years." Catherine rejoiced in saying.

"That's good news indeed!" Bode exhorted.

Camille suggested they not rush to judgement concerning Catherine's father as the circumstances were vastly different now.

As the Swafford's, Bode, and Catherine gathered at the bottom of the gangplank connecting to Ellis Island, they collectively scanned the departing passengers for any sign of Mr. Wolcott. After half an hour of inspecting the passengers leaving the ship, Charlie said that if Mr. Wolcott had indeed slipped ashore without notice he most likely would travel west, back to Denver and familiar territory.

The Swaffords would be staying on in New York to visit Camille's uncle, and Bode said he was unsure of his future plans.

"Would you grant me the pleasure of seeing you before your return to St. Anderew's to finish your schooling?" Bode requested of Catherine.

"I think that would be nice," she replied, and Bode's heart swelled with possibilities.

CHAPTER THIRTY-TWO
DADDY'S GIRL
Boston, Massachusetts, June 1937

Catherine was very happy to be home with her parents and glad that she and Bode Cuddling had parted on good terms. She liked him very much, and he promised to call on her in the next few days. She told her father about Harry Vardon's funeral, and when asked about the voyage home, she only said it was full of colorful characters. It was Saturday, and her mother was cleaning out the attic. Her mother called down to her father, who was reading the newspaper and sipping tea.

"Honey, do you want these old golf clubs? They've been sitting up here collecting dust for decades."

Her father removed his glasses, raised an eyebrow, and replied, "Oh no, you can have those old things thrown out."

Hearing that, Catherine's mother called down from the attic door, "Sweetie, would you please come over and take these golf clubs when I hand them down?"

Catherine put down the dish that she was drying on the kitchen counter and, after drying her hands, hurried over to accept the golf bag that was already halfway down through the attic opening. She took it in her arms.

"Got 'em!"

"Sweetie, just put them out by the trash bin for pickup. Maybe someone will just come and take them, although those old things aren't worth much to anybody."

"Why not?" Catherine casually called back over her shoulder.

"They're left-handed for one, sweetie!"

Catherine felt sick to her stomach and set the bag down by the trash bin, where she noticed the dusty name tag attached to the bag. She reached down and twisted it so that she could read it. On it was printed Walter Fairbanks, Overland Country Club, Denver, CO.

Catherine's mother was almost done cleaning the attic when she heard her daughter's footsteps ascending the stairs. She was so happy to have Catherine home. It wouldn't be long before she would graduate from Saint Andrew's University in Scotland and make her own way in the world.

"Mother, where are Daddy's journals?"

Catherine's mother turned around to face her daughter.

"Where is what, sweetie?"

"The journals describing the Jack the Ripper murders back in 1888."

Her mother remained silent.

"Well, if you don't know, then maybe Claire Davis does?" Catherine's mother dropped the dusty glass bowl she was holding, and it broke on the hardwood floor.

"Everything okay up there?" Catherine's father called up from the living room.

"So you know?" her mother said, lowering herself down on a crate.

"Is it all true?" Camille asked, but before her mother could answer, the front doorbell rang.

"That's Lilian, our neighbor, bringing back a mixing bowl," her mother said, pulling her head back up with tears in her eyes. "Your father saved my life and has saved countless lives as a doctor here in Boston for the last thirty years. It's true that for several months in 1888, your father was a very sick man, yet the demons inside his head that prompted those terrible crimes were gone by the time we left Denver in 1900. It's almost as if the day we left those memories were magically erased from his brain."

"I love Daddy, but what about justice for those poor women who he killed so viciously?"

"Darling, would you and Catherine please come down. I need to speak to you," Catherine's father hollered up the attic stairs.

"Oh my god, Mother, he's going to kill us!" Catherine gasped.

"Don't be ridiculous!" her mother said, rising from the crate and moving toward the attic door. "Not a word to your father that you know about his past. It would kill him!"

Camille and her mother reached the hallway landing, made their way down the hall, and turned into the living room, where they found Catherine's father chatting with Camille and Charlie Swafford. Camille quickly stood and made her way over to Catherine.

"Miss George, it's nice to see you again!" She took Catherine's hand in hers.

"Thank you, Mrs. Swafford; this is my mother." Camille shook Catherine's mother's hand.

"Ladies, please sit down. We were just catching up on some old times. Charlie and I go way back to when I briefly lived in London. We had tea one dreadful night and talked about golf among other things. They said they saw you at Harry Vardon's funeral and sailed home with you."

"That's right, Father; I completely forgot to tell you about the Swaffords, as all my thoughts have been directed toward a young man by the name of Bode Cuddling, who I also met on the ship."

"Darling, the name Cuddling is quite familiar," Catherine's mother interjected.

"Yes, Bode's father, JR, and I had quite a competition with the weights and a doozy of a wrestling match back in the day. If young Bode is anything like his father, I'd love to make his acquaintance."

The front doorbell rang again.

"Oh, that's Lilian returning a mixing bowl," Catherine's mother said, rising up.

"You stay there, darling, I'm closer to the door. I'll get it." Catherine's father got up and made his way to the door. As he pulled the door open, he called over his shoulder, "Charlie, tell Catherine about the Ten Bells Pub!"

A shot rang out, and Dr. George fell backward onto the floor with a deadening thud. Catherine's mother screamed, and everyone rushed to his side. On the other side of the door stood Henry Wolcott with a smoking pistol in his hand. The wound was a mortal one, and Dr. George's eyes were wide with fright, then suddenly changed to peaceful.

"Look, Charlie, there's Mary Jane Kelly! She's forgiven me and is extending her hand. Isn't she a peach, Charlie? Isn't she a peach?"

His eyes closed, and Jack the Ripper was no more.

The End

EPILOGUE

It was the stroke of midnight in 1937, the night Jack the Ripper was sent to his grave. The Bad Witch and the Good Witch were once again sitting before a fire, tending to a black cauldron containing a concoction some would describe as soup and others as a sorcerer's brew. The Good Witch asked the Evil Witch to hand over a small amount of eye of newt, which the Evil Witch did so reluctantly.

"By the way I heard from the wise old owl that you made an albatross the last time you played golf," said the Good Witch to the Bad Witch.

"Yes, I did, but no one believes me on account of—"

"Yes, I know, because you cheat a lot," replied the Good Witch.

"I know what you're up to," said the Bad Witch.

The Good Witch added the newt and began to stir with the heavy ladle. "Yes, you can begin to see; wait, just a few more stirs, and there it just came into focus. Slide over and have a look," the Good Witch requested, and the Bad Witch complied with a shrug of the shoulders.

"For all the pain and suffering you caused this time around, I was able to conjure up this silver lining."

"I hate it when you gloat," said the Bad Witch.

There, in the soupy liquid, appeared the vision of a young woman and man sitting on a swing that was located on a porch. Catherine and Body were together, and their affection was evident as they held hands, and she leaned her head on his shoulder.

"Maybe I should take that vacation," said the bad witch, "as I'm growing tired of your silver linings."

"Oh, come now; have some soup and be happy," said the Good Witch.

Sequel to *Albatross, Talons and Tears,* coming in the Fall

Milton Keynes UK
Ingram Content Group UK Ltd.
UKHW011834210624
444498UK00001B/104